CHAPTER II

THE ADVENTURES OF
PINOCCHIO

CARLO COLLODI

THE ADVENTURES OF

PINOCCHIO

Illustrated by
ROBERTO INNOCENTI

Translated by E. Harden

Alfred A. Knopf ❧ New York

THIS IS A BORZOI BOOK PUBLISHED BY ALFRED A. KNOPF, INC.

Translation copyright 1944 by the Estate of E. Harden.
Illustrations copyright © 1988 by Roberto Innocenti.
All rights reserved under International and Pan-American Copyright
Conventions. Published in the United States by Alfred A. Knopf, Inc.,
New York. Distributed by Random House, Inc., New York.
Originally published in Italian in 1882. This
translation was originally published in Australia by
Consolidated Press, 1944. This edition was
originally published in Great Britain
by Jonathan Cape Ltd., London.
Manufactured in Italy

1 3 5 7 9 0 8 6 4 2

Library of Congress Cataloging-in-Publication Data
Collodi, Carlo, 1826-1890. The adventures of Pinocchio.
Translation of: Le avventure di Pinocchio. Reprint.
Translation originally published in Australia by Consolidated Press,
1944. Illustrations c1988.
Summary: Pinocchio, a wooden puppet full of tricks and mischief,
with a talent for getting into and out of trouble, wants
more than anything else to become a real boy.
[1. Puppets—Fiction. 2. Fairy tales]
I. Innocenti, Roberto, ill. II. Title.
PZ8.C7Ph   1988b
[Fic]
88-8918
ISBN 0-394-82110-6

To Carlo Collodi and my daughter Alessandra

CHAPTER 1

*How it happened that Mr Cherry, the carpenter,
found a piece of wood that laughed
and cried like a child*

There was once upon a time. . .

"A king!" my little readers will shout together.

No, children, you make a mistake. Once upon a time there was a piece of wood.

It was not the best, but just a common piece of wood, such as is used in stoves and fireplaces to kindle the fire and warm the rooms in winter.

How it happened I cannot tell, but the fact is that one fine day this piece of wood just happened to be there in the shop of an old carpenter whose real name was Mr Antonio, but everyone called him Mr Cherry, because the tip of his nose was always as red and shiny as a ripe cherry.

As soon as Mr Cherry noticed this piece of wood, he was delighted. He rubbed his hands together joyfully and said, "This has come at exactly the right moment. It is just what I need to make a leg for my little table."

Then, without hesitating a moment, he took his sharp axe to strip off the bark and the rough part of the wood. But just as he raised the axe for the first blow, he stopped with his arm in the air, for he heard a very tiny voice, begging him gently, "Don't strike me too hard!"

You can imagine old Mr Cherry's surprise.

He looked round the room to see where the tiny voice had come from, but he saw nobody. He looked under the bench – nobody. He looked in the cupboard which was always shut; but there was nobody. He looked in the basket of chips and sawdust – no one. He opened the door and looked out into the street – no one! What was to be done?

"I see," he said at last, laughing and scratching his wig. "I must have imagined that tiny voice. Now let's to work!"

He raised his axe again, and down it went on the piece of wood.

"Oh, you hurt me!" complained the same tiny voice.

This time Mr Cherry was struck all of a heap. His eyes stood out of his head, his mouth was wide open, and his tongue hung out over his chin, as you see on some fountain masks.

As soon as he could speak he said, trembling and stuttering with fright, "But where did that tiny voice come from that cried 'Oh'? There's not a living soul here. Is it possible that this piece of wood has learnt to cry and complain like a baby? I can't believe it. This piece of wood – just look at it! It's nothing but a piece of firewood, like all the others; when you put it on the fire it will make a kettle boil. Well, then? Is someone hidden inside it? If there is, so much the worse for him. I'll attend to him!"

And he took the poor piece of wood in both hands and, without mercy, started to beat it against the wall.

Then he stopped and listened to hear if any tiny voice were complaining this time. He waited two minutes – nothing; five minutes – nothing; ten minutes – and still nothing!

"Now I understand!" he exclaimed, laughing and pulling his wig. "I must have imagined that tiny voice that said 'Oh!' I'd better do my work." And, because he was very frightened, he began singing to encourage himself.

Meanwhile he put the axe down and taking his plane, began planing and shaping the piece of wood.

But while the plane went to and fro, he again heard that tiny voice which said, laughing, "Stop! you're tickling me!"

This time, poor Mr Cherry dropped as if struck by lightning.

When he opened his eyes, he was sitting on the floor. He was so changed you could hardly have recognized him. Even the end of his nose, which was always red, had turned blue with fright.

CHAPTER 2

*Mr Cherry gives the piece of wood to his friend,
Geppetto, who plans a marvellous puppet that can dance,
and fence, and turn somersaults in the air*

At that moment somebody knocked on the door. "Come in!" said the carpenter; but he was too weak to stand up.

A little, jolly old man came into the shop. His name was Geppetto, but when the boys in the neighbourhood wanted to tease him they called him by his nickname of Polendina, because of his yellow wig which looked very like a dish of polenta.*

Geppetto was very short-tempered. Woe betide anybody who called him Polendina! He simply went wild, and no one could do anything with him.

"Good morning, Mr Antonio," said Geppetto. "What are you doing down there?"

"I am teaching the ants how to read."

"Much good may it do you!"

"What brought you here, Mr Geppetto?"

"My legs. Mr Antonio, I have come to ask you a favour."

"Here I am, ready to serve you," answered the carpenter, getting to his knees.

"I had an idea this morning."

"Let us hear it."

"I thought I would make a fine wooden puppet – a really fine one, that can dance, fence, and turn somersaults in the air. Then, with this puppet, I could travel round the world, and earn my bit of bread and my glass of wine. What do you think about it?"

"Bravo, Polendina!" cried that same tiny, mysterious voice.

When he heard the name Polendina, Mr Geppetto became so angry that he turned as red as a ripe pepper. He turned to the carpenter, and said in a fury, "Why do you annoy me?"

"Who is annoying you?"

"You called me Polendina!"

"No, I didn't!"

"Oh! Perhaps I did it! But I say that it was you."

"No!"

"Yes!"

"No!"

*A pudding made of maize (Indian corn).

"Yes!"

And, as they grew more and more excited, from words they came to blows. They seized one another's wigs, and even hit and bit and scratched each other.

At the end of the fight Geppetto's yellow wig was in Mr Antonio's hands, and the carpenter's grey wig between Geppetto's teeth.

"Give me my wig!" said Mr Antonio.

"You give me mine, and let us make a peace treaty!"

So the two little old men, each taking his own wig, shook hands, and promised to be good friends for ever.

"Now, neighbour Geppetto," said the carpenter, to prove that they were friends again, "what can I do for you?"

"I would like to have a little piece of wood to make my marionette. Will you give it to me?"

Mr Antonio, pleased as Punch, hurried to his bench, and took the piece of wood which had frightened him so much. But, just as he was giving it to his friend, it shook so hard that it slipped out of his hands, and struck poor Geppetto's shin.

"Ah! This is a fine way to make me a present, Mr Antonio! You have almost lamed me."

"Upon my honour, I didn't do it!"

"Oh! So *I* did it then!"

"It's all the fault of this piece of wood —"

"Yes, I know the wood hit me, but you threw it at my legs!"

"I did not throw it at you!"

"That's a lie!"

"Geppetto, don't insult me! If you do, I shall call you Polendina."

"Blockhead!"

"Polendina!"

"Donkey!"

"Polendina!"

"Ugly monkey!"

"Polendina!"

When he heard himself called Polendina for the third time Geppetto, blind with rage, rushed at the carpenter, and the second fight was worse than the first.

When it was over, Mr Antonio had two more scratches on his nose, and Geppetto two buttons less on his jacket. Honours thus being even, they shook hands again, and vowed to be good friends for ever. Then Geppetto took the piece of wood and, thanking Mr Antonio, went limping home.

CHAPTER 3

Geppetto goes home and makes his puppet;
he calls him Pinocchio;
the puppet gets into mischief

eppetto's little room on the ground floor was lit by a window under the stairs. His furniture could not have been simpler. An old chair, a tottering bed, and a broken-down table. At the back of the room you could see a fireplace, with the fire lit; but the fire was painted, and over the fire was painted a kettle boiling merrily, with a cloud of steam that was just like real steam.

As soon as he arrived home, Geppetto took his tools and began to make his puppet.

"What shall I call him?" he asked himself. "I think I shall call him Pinocchio. That name will bring him good luck. I once knew a whole family of Pinocchios: there was Pinocchio the father, and Pinocchia the mother, and Pinocchii the children, and they all got along splendidly. The richest of them was a beggar."

Having thought out a name for his puppet, he started his work with great determination. He made his hair, his forehead, and his eyes in a very short time.

As soon as the eyes were finished, imagine his bewilderment when he saw them moving and looking at him!

When Geppetto saw those two wooden eyes looking at him, he did not like it at all, and he said angrily, "Naughty wooden eyes, why are you staring at me?"

But no one answered.

After the eyes, he made the nose; but as soon as it was finished, it began to grow. It grew, and it grew, and in a few minutes' time it was as long as if there was no end to it.

Poor Geppetto worked fast to shorten it; but the more he cut it off, the longer that insolent nose became.

After the nose, he made the mouth; but before he had finished it, it began to laugh and poke fun at him.

"Stop laughing!" said Geppetto; but he might as well have spoken to the wall.

"Stop laughing, I say!" he shouted, menacingly.

The mouth stopped laughing, and stuck out its tongue.

However, as Geppetto did not want to spoil the puppet, he pretended not to see it, and continued his work.

After the mouth, he made the chin, then the neck, the shoulders, the stomach, the arms, and the hands.

As soon as the hands were finished, Geppetto's wig was snatched from his head. He looked up, and what should he see but his yellow wig in the puppet's hands.

"Pinocchio! Give me back my wig at once!"

But Pinocchio, instead of giving back the wig, put it on his own head, and was almost hidden under it.

This cheeky, mocking behaviour made Geppetto feel sadder than ever before in his life. He turned to Pinocchio, and said, "You scoundrel of a son! You are not even finished, and you already disobey your father! That's bad, my boy – very bad!" And he wiped away a tear.

There were still the legs and feet to make.

When Geppetto had finished the feet, he received a kick on the nose.

"It serves me right," he said to himself. "I should have thought of it before. Now it is too late."

He took the puppet in his hands, and put him down on the floor to see if he could walk; but Pinocchio's legs were stiff, and he did not know how to move them. So Geppetto led him by the hand, and showed him how to put one foot before the other.

When the stiffness went out of his legs, Pinocchio started to walk alone, and run around the room; and finally he slipped through the door into the street and ran away.

Poor old Geppetto ran after him as quickly as he could, but he did not catch him, for the little rascal jumped like a rabbit, and his wooden feet clattered on the pavement, making as much noise as twenty pairs of wooden shoes.

"Catch him! Catch him!" cried Geppetto.

But when the people saw that wooden puppet running as fast as a racehorse, they looked at him in amazement, and then laughed, and laughed, and laughed, until their sides were aching.

At last, by some lucky chance, a policeman came and when he heard the clatter, he thought somebody's horse had run away from its master. So he courageously stood in the middle of the street with his legs apart, in order to stop it, and prevent any more trouble.

From far away, Pinocchio saw the policeman barricading the street, and he decided to run between his legs; but he failed dismally.

The policeman, without moving from his place, picked him up by the nose – that ridiculous, long nose, that seemed made on purpose to be caught by policemen – and returned him to Geppetto, who wanted to pull his ears to punish him for his naughtiness. Imagine what he felt when he could not find any ears! And do you know why? Because he had made him in such a hurry that he had forgotten his ears.

So he took him by the nape of his neck, and as they walked away he said, shaking his head menacingly, "You just come home, and I'll settle your account when we get there!"

At this threatening remark, Pinocchio threw himself down on the ground, and refused to walk.

A crowd of idle and inquisitive people gathered around him. Some said one thing, some another.

"The poor puppet," said some of them, "is right, not wanting to go home! Who knows how horribly that bad Geppetto might beat him?"

And others added, with evil tongues, "Geppetto *seems* to be a good man, but he is a perfect tyrant with children. If we leave that poor marionette in his hands, he may tear him to pieces."

In short, so much was said and done that the policeman let Pinocchio go, and

decided to take poor Geppetto to prison.

He could not, for the time being, say anything in his own defence, but he cried like a calf and, as they walked towards the prison, he whimpered, "Wretched son! And to think that I worked so hard to make a fine puppet! But serve me right. I ought to have known what would happen!"

What happened afterwards is almost too much to believe and I shall tell you about it in the following chapters.

CHAPTER 4

The story of Pinocchio and the talking cricket
in which we see that naughty children
do not like to be corrected by those who
are wiser than they are

ell, I must tell you children, that while poor Geppetto was led to prison through no fault of his own, that rascal Pinocchio, left alone, ran home across the fields as quickly as possible. In his hurry he jumped over high banks, thorn hedges, and ditches full of water, like a kid, or a young hare running away from the hunters.

When he arrived home, he found the door ajar. Pushing it open he went in, and locked it securely after him. Then he threw himself down on the ground with a great sigh of relief.

But the relief did not last long, for he heard someone in the room saying, *"Cri-cri-cri!"*

"Who is calling me?" said Pinocchio, frightened.

"It is I."

Pinocchio turned and saw a big cricket creeping up the wall. "Tell me, cricket, who are you?"

"I am the talking cricket, and I have lived in this room a hundred years or more."

"But now this is my room, and you will oblige me by going away at once, without even turning round."

"I shall not leave," replied the cricket, "until I have told you a great truth."

"Well then, tell me, and be quick about it!"

"Woe to those boys who revolt against their parents, and run away from home. They will never do any good in this world, and sooner or later they will repent bitterly."

"Sing away, cricket, just as long as you please! But as for me, tomorrow at sunrise I am going to leave; for if I stay here the same will happen to me as happens to other boys: I shall be sent to school, and one way or other, by love or by force, I shall be made to study."

"You poor fool! Don't you know that, if you spend your time like that, you will grow up to be a great donkey, and everyone will make fun of you?"

"Be quiet, you good for nothing, croaking cricket!" shouted Pinocchio.

But the cricket, who was patient, and a philosopher too, instead of being offended by such impudence, continued in the same tone, "But if you don't like to go to school, why don't you learn a trade, so that you may at least earn your bread honestly?"

"Do you want me to tell you something?" answered Pinocchio, beginning to lose his patience. "Of all the trades in the world, there is only one which really attracts me."

"And what might that be?"

"To eat, drink, sleep, and amuse myself, and to lead a vagabond life from morning to night."

"Let me tell you," said the talking cricket, as calm as ever, "that those who follow that trade finish, nearly always, in a hospital or in prison."

"Be careful, you cricket of ill omen! If you make me angry, woe betide you!"

"Poor Pinocchio! I am really sorry for you!"

"Why are you sorry for me?"

"Because you are a puppet, and – what is worse – you have a wooden head."

At these last words Pinocchio lost his temper and, seizing a mallet from the bench, threw it at the cricket.

Perhaps he did not mean to hit him, but unfortunately the mallet struck him right on the head. The poor cricket had scarcely time to cry *"Cri-cri-cri"*, and there he was, stretched out stiff, and flattened against the wall.

CHAPTER 5

Pinocchio is hungry, and he looks for an egg
to make himself an omelette;
but just as he breaks it in the pan
the omelette flies through the window

It was growing dark, and Pinocchio remembered that he had eaten nothing all day. There was a painful feeling in his stomach that closely resembled appetite.

With boys appetite grows fast. In fact, after a few minutes his appetite became hunger, and in no time he was as hungry as a wolf. His hunger was unbearable.

Poor Pinocchio hurried to the fireplace where a kettle was boiling and put out his hand to lift the lid and see what was in it; but the kettle was only painted on the wall. Imagine his disappointment! His nose, which was already too long, grew three inches longer.

He ran about the room, searched in every cupboard and in every possible place for a little bread – even dry bread. He would have been grateful for a crust, or a bone left by a dog, for a fishbone or a cherry stone – in short, for anything he could chew. But he found nothing, just nothing, absolutely nothing.

He kept growing hungrier every moment, yet he could do nothing but yawn. He yawned so tremendously that his mouth reached his ears; and after he yawned he spattered, and he felt as if he hadn't any stomach left.

At last, in despair, he began to cry, saying, "The talking cricket was right. I did wrong to revolt against my father and run away from home. If my father were here now, I shouldn't be dying of yawning. Oh, hunger is a dreadful illness!"

Suddenly, in a rubbish heap, he noticed something white and round that looked like an egg. In less than no time he grabbed it. It really was an egg.

To describe his joy would be impossible; you can only imagine it. He feared he might be dreaming. He turned the egg from one hand to the other, and patted it and kissed it as he said, "Now, how shall I cook it? Shall I make an omelette? No, it would be better to poach it. But perhaps it would be more tasty if I fried it in a pan. Or shall I just boil it in the shell? No, the quickest way would be to poach it. I am just dying to eat it."

Without further ado, he set a stewing pan over a brazier of red charcoal. Instead of oil or butter, he put some water in it and when the water began to boil – tac! he broke the eggshell and held it over the pan that the contents might drop into it.

But instead of the yolk and white of an egg, a little chicken flew out and, making a polite curtsy, said gaily, "A thousand thanks, Master Pinocchio, for having spared me the trouble of breaking the shell! Take care of yourself, and give my love to the folks at home. I hope to see you again."

With that, the chicken spread its wings and, flying through the open window, was soon lost to sight.

The poor puppet stood there as if bewitched, with his eyes fixed and his mouth open. When he recovered a little from his first bewilderment, he began to cry, and scream, and stamp on the floor in despair; and as he sobbed he said, "Indeed, the talking cricket was right. If I hadn't run away from home, and if my father were here, I should not now be dying of hunger. Oh, hunger is a dreadful illness!"

His stomach was complaining more than ever and, as he did not know how to quieten it, he decided to go out again into the village, in the hope of meeting some charitable person who would give him some bread.

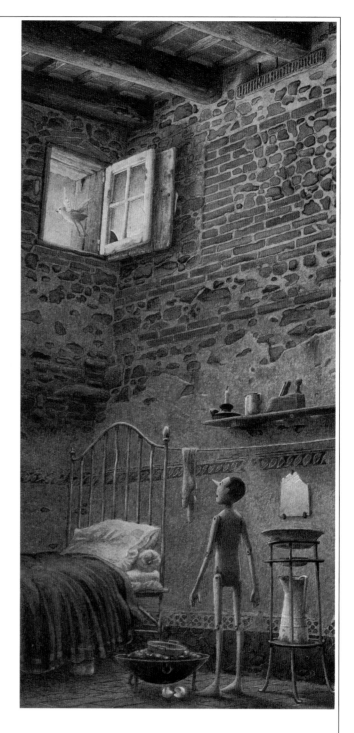

CHAPTER 6

*Pinocchio falls asleep with his feet
on the brazier, and,
when he wakes up in the morning,
finds them burnt off*

It was a windy, cold night. The thunder was fierce and the lightning as violent as though the sky was on fire. A bitter wind whistled angrily, raising clouds of dust and making the trees tremble and groan.

Pinocchio was frightened of thunder, but he was still more hungry than frightened; so he opened the door, and ran as fast as he could to the village, which he soon reached, panting, with his tongue hanging out like a hunting dog's.

But all was dark and quiet. The shops were closed, the doors and windows shut, and there was not even a dog in the street. It seemed a village of the dead.

However Pinocchio, driven by hunger and despair, gave a very long peal at the doorbell of one of the houses, saying to himself, "This will bring somebody out."

And indeed, a little old man with a nightcap on his head came to a window, and shouted angrily, "What do you want at this hour?"

"Will you be so kind as to give me some bread?"

"Wait! I'll be back at once!" said the old man, believing that he had to

21

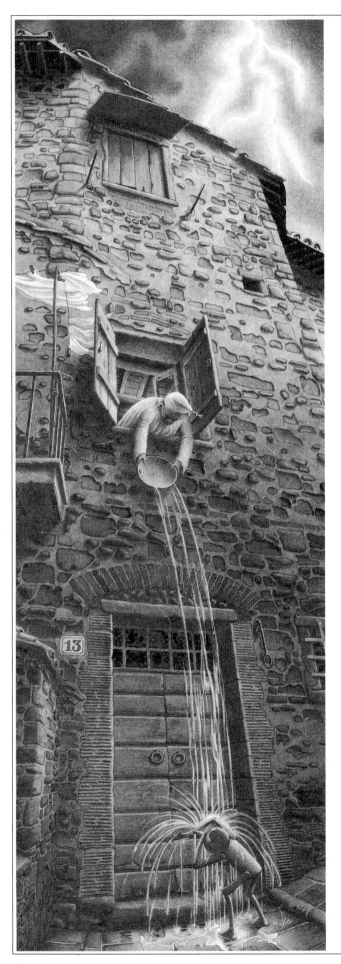

do with one of those street urchins who amuse themselves at night by ringing doorbells, and rousing good people who are sleeping peacefully.

In half a minute a window was opened, and the same voice called Pinocchio, "Stand under the window, and hold out your hand!"

Pinocchio held out his hands, and a great basin of water poured down on him, drenching him from head to foot, as if he had been a pot of dry geraniums.

He went home wet as a rag, and exhausted with fatigue and hunger. He had no strength to stand, and so he sat down, and put his wet, muddy feet on the brazier full of burning coal.

Then he fell asleep, and while he was asleep his feet, which were wooden, caught fire, and slowly burned away to cinders.

Pinocchio slept and snored, as though his feet belonged to someone else. At last, at daybreak, he was awakened by someone rapping on the door.

"Who is it?" he called, yawning, and rubbing his eyes.

"It is I!" answered a voice.

And it was the voice of Geppetto.

CHAPTER 7

Geppetto comes home,
and gives Pinocchio the breakfast that
the poor man had brought for himself

oor Pinocchio's eyes were still half closed, and he had not noticed that his feet were burnt off. Thus, when he heard his father's voice, he tumbled down from his stool to run and open the door; but, after staggering a couple of times, he fell his full length on the floor, making a noise as of a whole bag of wooden ladles falling from the fifth storey.

"Open the door!" cried Geppetto from the street.

"I can't, daddy," answered the marionette, crying, and rolling over and over on the floor.

"Why not?"

"Because somebody has eaten my feet!"

"And who has eaten them?"

"The cat," said Pinocchio, seeing the cat who was just then playing with some shavings with his forepaws.

"Open the door, I tell you!" Geppetto cried again. "If you don't, I'll give you the cat-o'-nine tails when I get in!"

"Believe me, I can't stand up. Oh, poor me! Poor me! I shall have to walk on my knees for the rest of my life!"

Geppetto, thinking that all this complaint was just another of Pinocchio's tricks, decided to end it for good. He climbed up the wall, and got in at the window.

At first he was angry, and scolded him; but, when he saw his own Pinocchio lying on the floor, and really without feet, his anger vanished.

He took him in his arms, kissed and caressed him, spoke many affectionate words and, with tears on his cheeks, he said, sobbing, "My dear little Pinocchio, how did you burn your feet?"

"I don't know, daddy. But believe me, it has been a horrid night. I shall never forget it as long as I live. It thundered and lightninged, and I was very hungry, and the talking cricket said, 'It serves you right; you have been wicked and you deserve it!' And I said, 'Be careful, cricket!' And he said, 'You are a puppet, and you have a wooden head!' And I threw the mallet at him, and he died; but it was his fault, for I didn't want to kill him. And the proof of that is that I put the pan on the brazier, but the chicken flew away and said, 'Good-bye, I shall see you again. Give my love to the folks!' And I got more and more hungry; and for that reason the little old man with the nightcap opened the window, and said, 'Stand under the window and hold out your hand!' And I got a basinful of water on my head. It isn't a disgrace to ask for a bit of bread, is it? I ran back home as quick as I could; and because I was so very hungry, I put my feet on the brazier to dry them. And then you came home, and I felt that my feet were burnt off, and I'm still so hungry, but I have no more feet! Boo-hoo-hoo!'' And poor Pinocchio began to cry and scream so loudly that he could have been heard five miles away.

Geppetto had only understood one thing of all this jumble of words – that Pinocchio was dying of hunger.

He took three pears out of his pocket, and said, giving them to him, "These three pears were for my breakfast, but I willingly give them to you. Eat them, and may they do you good!"

"If you want me to eat them, kindly peel them for me."

"Peel them for you?" cried Geppetto, astonished. "I would never have thought, my lad, that you were so refined and fastidious. That's too bad! We should get used, from childhood, to eating everything, and liking it; for one never knows what might happen in this curious world."

"That's all very well," retorted Pinocchio, "but I'll never eat fruit that isn't peeled. I can't stand skins."

So that patient, kind Geppetto took a knife and peeled the three pears, putting all the peelings on the corner of the table.

When Pinocchio had eaten the first pear in two mouthfuls, he was about to throw away the core, but Geppetto stopped him.

"Don't throw it away! There might be some use for it."

"Can you imagine I shall ever eat the core?" cried Pinocchio, turning on him in a rage.

"Who knows! This is a curious world," replied Geppetto, calmly.

So the three cores, instead of being thrown out of the window, were placed on the corner of the table together with the parings.

When he had eaten, or rather devoured the three pears, Pinocchio yawned, and then began to whimper, "I'm still hungry."

"But, my son, I have nothing more to give you."

"Nothing? Nothing at all?"

"Only the peelings and cores you left."

"All right!" said Pinocchio. "If there's really nothing else, I might eat some peelings."

And he began promptly. At first he made faces; but, one after another, he quickly ate all the peelings; and after them the cores. And when he had eaten everything, he clapped his stomach and said cheerfully, "Now I feel better!"

"You see," said Geppetto, "I was right when I said you should not be so refined and fastidious about your food. My dear boy, we never know what might happen to us. This is a curious world."

CHAPTER 8

*Geppetto makes Pinocchio new feet,
and sells his own coat to buy him a primer*

As soon as the marionette had satisfied his hunger, he began to cry and grumble because he wanted new feet.

But Geppetto, in order to punish him for all his naughtiness, let him cry and complain for half a day. Then he said, "Why should I make you new feet? So that you may escape from home again?"

"I promise," said the marionette, sobbing, "that from now on I'll be good."

"All children, when they want something, tell the same story," replied Geppetto.

"I promise to go to school, and study, and do my best as a good boy should –"

"All children, when they want something, say the same thing."

"But I'm not like other children! I'm better than all of them, and I always tell the truth. I promise you, daddy, that I shall learn a trade, and be the staff and comfort of your old age."

Geppetto tried to look very severe; but his eyes were full of tears, and his heart was full of sadness when he saw his poor Pinocchio in such a dreadful state. He did not say another word, but, taking his tools and two little pieces of seasoned wood, he set to work as hard as he could.

In less than an hour the feet were ready – two well-shaped, nimble, swift little feet that might have been carved by a great artist.

Then Geppetto said to Pinocchio, "Shut your eyes and go to sleep."

Pinocchio shut his eyes, and pretended to be asleep. And while he did so Geppetto, with some glue melted in an eggshell, fastened the feet in place; and he did it so neatly that no one could even see where they were joined together. As soon as Pinocchio discovered he had his feet again, he jumped down from the table where he was lying and began to gambol and dance around the room, nearly mad with joy.

"Now, to prove to you how grateful I am," said Pinocchio to his father, "I want to go to school at once."

"What a good boy!"

"But if I'm going to school, I must have some clothes."

Geppetto, who was poor and had not a farthing in his pocket, made Pinocchio a suit out of flowered paper, a pair of shoes out of bark from a tree, and a hat out of bread.

Pinocchio ran to look at himself in a basin of water; and he was so pleased with himself that he said, as he strutted about, "I look exactly like a gentleman!"

"Yes, indeed," answered Geppetto, "but remember, it is not fine clothes that make a gentleman, but clean clothes."

"By the way, speaking of school," added Pinocchio, "there's still something I must have – the most necessary of all."

"And that is . . .?"

"I have no primer."

"That's right. But how shall I get one?"

"That's easy! Go to the bookseller and buy one."

"And the money?"

"I haven't any."

"Neither have I," added the good old man, sadly.

Pinocchio, although he was usually very cheerful, became sad, too; for poverty, when it is real poverty, destroys all joy, even in children.

"Wait," Geppetto cried suddenly and, jumping up, he put on his old coat, full of holes and patches, and ran out of the shop.

In a little while he was back again, with a primer in his hand for Pinocchio. But the poor man was in his shirt-sleeves, and it was snowing outside.

"Where is your coat, daddy?"

"I have sold it."

"Why did you sell it?"

"Because it made me too warm."

Pinocchio understood this answer instantly; and he was so overcome by the feelings of his good heart, that he threw his arms around Geppetto's neck and kissed him again and again.

CHAPTER 9

*Pinocchio sells his primer that he may go
and see the marionettes*

When it stopped snowing, Pinocchio started for school with his fine new primer under his arm. On the way, he never stopped imagining all sorts of fine plans, and he built a thousand castles in the air, each one more beautiful than the other.

He began by saying to himself, "At school today I shall learn to read in no time; tomorrow I shall learn to write, and the day after tomorrow I shall learn all the figures. Then I shall be clever enough to earn lots of money; and with the very first money I get I shall buy my father the nicest, new, cloth coat. But why cloth? It shall be made of gold and silver, with diamond buttons. That poor man really deserves it; for, that I should be a learned man, he sold his coat to buy me a book – in this cold weather, too! Only fathers can make such sacrifices."

While he was saying this more and more excitedly, he thought he heard music in the distance that sounded like fife and drum: *fi-fi-fi . . . zum, zum, zum, zum.*

He stopped and listened. The sounds came from the end of the street that crossed the one which led to school, at the end of the little village near the sea.

"What can that music be? What a pity I have to go to school! Otherwise . . ." He hesitated, deciding whether to go to school or listen to the fifes.

"Today I shall listen to the fifes, and tomorrow I shall go to school," this naughty boy said finally, shrugging his shoulders.

No sooner said than done. He ran, and the farther he ran the more distinctly

he heard the tune of the fifes and the beating of the big drum: *fi-fi-fi, fi-fi-fi, . . . zum, zum, zum.*

At last he came to a little square full of people who were gathered around a great building of boards and cloth, painted in all colours of the rainbow.

"What is that big building?" Pinocchio asked a boy who seemed to live there.

"Read the poster – it is all written there – and then you'll know."

"I'd gladly read it, but I don't know how to read today."

"Bravo, nincompoop! I'll read it for you. Know, then, that on that big poster, in fiery red letters, is written: GREAT PUPPET SHOW."

"Is it long since the play began?"

"It's just beginning now."

"How much does it cost to go in?"

"Twopence."

Pinocchio was in such a fever of curiosity that he lost his self-control and without any shame, he said to the little boy, "Will you lend me twopence until tomorrow?"

"I'd simply love to," said the boy, laughing at him, "but I can't today."

"I shall sell you my jacket for twopence," said the puppet.

"What could I do with a jacket of flowered paper? If it should rain and got wet, I couldn't take it off."

"Will you buy my shoes?"

"They're only good for lighting a fire."

"What will you give me for my hat?"

"That would be a fine bargain! A hat made of bread! The mice might eat it right off my head!"

Pinocchio was sitting on horns. He was almost ready to make one more offer, but he had not the courage. He hesitated, but at last he said, "Will you buy this new primer for twopence?"

"I am only a boy, and I do not buy anything from other boys," said the other, having more sense than the puppet.

"I'll give you twopence for the primer," cried an old-clothes dealer who had overheard the conversation.

The book was sold at once. And to think that poor Geppetto stayed at home shivering in his shirt-sleeves, because he had to sell his coat to buy that primer for his son!

CHAPTER 10

*The puppets recognize Pinocchio as one of them,
and are pleased to see him, but Fire-eater,
the Showman, appears in the midst of their joy,
and Pinocchio almost comes to a bad end*

hen Pinocchio entered the puppet show, he nearly caused a revolution. You must know that the curtain was up, and they had just started the play.

Harlequin and Punchinello were on the stage, quarrelling as usual, threatening every moment to come to blows.

The audience paid the closest attention, and were laughing until they were sore to see those two puppets quarrelling and gesticulating and calling each other names, just as if they were truly two reasoning beings, two real persons.

But all at once Harlequin stopped and, turning to the public, pointed to the pit of the theatre, and shouted dramatically:

"Heavens above! Am I awake, or am I dreaming? That must be Pinocchio there!"

"Yes, it's indeed Pinocchio!" cried Punchinello.

"It is indeed!" exclaimed Miss Rosy, peeping from the back of the stage.

"Here's Pinocchio! Here's Pinocchio!" shouted all the puppets in chorus, running to the stage from every wing. "Here's Pinocchio! Here's our brother Pinocchio! Hurrah for Pinocchio!"

"Come up here to me, Pinocchio!" cried Harlequin. "Come and throw yourself into the arms of your wooden brothers!"

At this affectionate invitation, Pinocchio made one jump from the back of the pit to the front seats. Another jump, and he landed on the head of the orchestra leader; and from there he jumped to the stage.

It is impossible to describe the hugging and kissing that followed, the friendly pinches, the brotherly taps that Pinocchio received from the actors and actresses of that puppet company.

It was a very spectacular sight, but the audience, when they saw that the play had stopped, grew impatient and began shouting, "The play! We want the play! Go on with the play!"

However, their breath was wasted, for the puppets, instead of continuing the play, redoubled their noise and, placing Pinocchio on their shoulders, carried him in triumph before the footlights.

Suddenly the Showman appeared. He was very tall, and so ugly that he frightened anyone who looked at him. His beard was like black ink, and it was

31

so long that it reached the ground. Believe me, he stepped on it when he walked. His mouth was as big as an oven, his eyes were like two burning red lanterns, and he was constantly cracking a great whip made of serpents and foxes' tails, twisted together.

When the Showman appeared so unexpectedly, everybody was speechless. No one breathed. You could have heard a fly in the air. Even the poor puppets, male and female, trembled like so many leaves.

"Why have you come here to disturb my theatre?" he asked Pinocchio, in a voice like that of a spook with a bad cold in his head.

"Believe me, Your Honour, it was not my fault."

"Not another word! We shall settle our accounts tonight."

As soon as the show was over, the Showman went into the kitchen, where the whole sheep, which he was preparing for his supper, was roasting on the slowly turning spit.

When he saw that there was not enough wood to finish roasting it, he called Harlequin and Punchinello and said, "Bring me in Pinocchio! You will find him hanging on a nail. He is made of nice, dry wood, and I am sure he will make a good fire for my roast."

At first Harlequin and Punchinello hesitated; but, when the Showman glanced at them menacingly, they obeyed. In a few moments they returned to the kitchen carrying poor Pinocchio, who was wriggling like an eel out of water, and shouting desperately:

"O daddy, O daddy, save me! I don't want to die. I don't want to die!"

CHAPTER 11

Fire-eater sneezes and pardons Pinocchio,
who later saves the life of his friend Harlequin

ire-eater, for that was the Showman's name, looked a horrid man, there can be no doubt about it, particularly with his black beard hanging down like an apron, covering his chest and legs. Yet at heart, he was really not so bad. When he saw poor Pinocchio struggling, and crying, "I don't want to die! I don't want to die!" he felt sorry for him and, although he tried not to, at last he could not help it and sneezed violently.

Harlequin, who had been sad and downhearted, and looking like a weeping willow, when he heard that sneeze, became cheerful, and bending towards Pinocchio, whispered, "Good news, brother! The Showman has sneezed. That's a sign that he's pitying you, and you are saved."

For you must know that, whilst other men weep, or at least pretend to wipe their eyes, when they pity somebody, whenever Fire-eater really pitied anyone, he had the habit of sneezing.

After the Showman had sneezed, he continued speaking gruffly, and shouted at Pinocchio, "Can't you stop crying? It gives me a nasty feeling in my stomach. I feel such a pain that . . . that . . . Atchoo! Atchoo!" – and this time he sneezed twice.

"God bless you!" said Pinocchio.

"Thank you. And your father and mother, are they alive?" asked Fire-eater.

"My father is, but I never knew my mother."

"Who knows how sorry your old father would be if I threw you on the fire! Poor old man! I pity him. A-tchoo! A-tchoo! A-tchoo!" – and he sneezed three times.

"Bless you!" cried Pinocchio.

"Thank you. But on the other hand, you must be sorry for me, too, because, as you see, I haven't enough wood to finish roasting my mutton – and believe me, you certainly would have been very useful. But now I have spared you, and I must not complain. Instead of you, I shall burn some puppet of my company under the spit. Come on, gendarmes!"

Two wooden gendarmes appeared immediately at this command. They were very tall, and very thin. They wore tricorne hats, and carried drawn swords in their hands.

The Showman ordered them hoarsely, "Take that Harlequin, bind him strongly and throw him on the fire. My mutton must be well roasted!"

Imagine poor Harlequin! He was so frightened that his legs bent under him, and he fell on his face.

At this heart-breaking sight, Pinocchio knelt down at the Showman's feet and, weeping, he soused with tears the whole length of his long beard. Then he pleaded, "Have mercy, Sir Fire-eater!"

"There are no sirs here!" replied the Showman, sternly.

"Have mercy, cavalier!"

"There are no cavaliers here!"

"Have mercy, commander!"

"There are no commanders here!"

"Have mercy, Your Excellency!"

When he heard himself called Your Excellency, the Showman smiled with his lips and, suddenly growing kind and calmer, asked Pinocchio, "Well, what can I do for you?"

"I implore you to pardon poor Harlequin!"

"It cannot be done. As I pardoned you, I must put him on the fire, for my mutton must be well roasted."

"In that case," cried Pinocchio, rising and throwing away his hat of bread, "in that case, I know my duty. Forward, gendarmes! Bind me and throw me in the fire! It is not just that poor Harlequin, my truest friend, should die for me.''

These words, shouted in a loud, heroic voice, caused all the marionettes present to weep. Even the gendarmes, although made of wood, cried like newborn babies.

At first Fire-eater remained as hard and cold as ice: slowly he began to melt, and to sneeze. When he had sneezed four or five times, he opened his arms affectionately to Pinocchio, saying, ''You are a good, brave boy! Come here, and give me a kiss.''

Pinocchio ran quickly and, climbing up the Showman's beard like a squirrel, gave him a loud kiss on the tip of his nose.

''And is my life spared?'' asked poor Harlequin, in a trembling voice that could hardly be heard.

''Your life is spared,'' replied Fire-eater. Then he added, shaking his head, ''Very well, then! This evening I must eat my mutton half done; but another time, woe to him who . . .!''

When they knew that their brothers were pardoned, all the puppets ran back to the stage, lit all the lights as for a festive performance, and began to jump and dance. They were still dancing at dawn.

CHAPTER 12

*Fire-eater gives Pinocchio five pieces of gold
to take to his father Geppetto:
but Pinocchio is deceived by the fox and the cat,
and goes away with them*

The next day Fire-eater called Pinocchio aside and asked him, "What is your father's name?"

"Geppetto."

"And what is his trade?"

"That of a very poor man."

"Does he earn very much?"

"He earns as much as he needs for never having a farthing in his pocket. Just imagine, in order to buy a primer for my schooling, he had to sell his only coat: a coat that was so full of holes and patches that it was shameful."

"Poor fellow! I am almost sorry for him. Here are five gold pieces. Hurry up and give them to him, with my compliments."

As you can well imagine, Pinocchio thanked the Showman a thousand times. One after another he embraced all the puppets of the company, even the gendarmes; then, almost beside himself with joy, he set out for home.

But before he had gone far he met a fox who was lame in one foot, and a cat who was blind in both eyes, getting along as best they could, like good companions in misfortune. The fox, who was lame, was leaning on the cat: and the cat, who was blind, was guided by the fox.

"Good morning, Pinocchio," said the fox, approaching politely.

"How do you know my name?" asked the puppet.

"I know your father well."

"Where did you see him?"

"I saw him yesterday, at the gate of his house."

"And what was he doing?"

"He was in his shirt-sleeves, and trembling with cold."

"Poor daddy! But never mind! From now on, he will shiver no more."

"Why not?"

"Because I am now a rich man."

"You? A rich man?" said the fox. And he began to laugh rudely and scornfully.

The cat laughed, too; but to hide it, she stroked her whiskers with her forepaws.

"There's nothing to laugh at," cried Pinocchio angrily. "I'm really sorry if what I say whets your appetite, but as you can see, there – if you understand such things – are five gold pieces." And he showed the money that Fire-eater had given him.

At the fascinating ringing of gold, the fox made an involuntary movement with the paw that seemed lame, and the cat opened wide her two blind eyes, but shut them again so quickly that Pinocchio did not notice.

"And now," asked the fox, "what are you going to do with the money?"

"First of all," answered the marionette, "I shall buy a beautiful new coat for my father – a coat made of gold and silver, and with diamond buttons. Then I will buy myself a primer."

"For yourself?"

"Of course; for I mean to go to school and study hard."

"Look at me," said the fox. "It is because of my foolish passion for study that I lost the use of my leg."

"And look at me," said the cat. "Because of *my* foolish passion for study, I lost the sight of both my eyes."

At that very moment, a white blackbird that was sitting on a hedge by the road sang its usual song, and said, "Pinocchio, don't listen to the advice of evil companions. If you do, you'll regret it."

Poor blackbird, if only he had not said it! The cat, with a great leap, jumped upon him and, without giving him time to say "oh", swallowed him in a mouthful, feathers and all.

Having devoured him she wiped her mouth, shut her eyes and shammed blindness as before.

"Poor blackbird!" said Pinocchio. "Why did you treat him so?"

"I did it to give him a lesson. He will learn not to be meddlesome again, when other people are talking."

They had gone nearly half-way towards Pinocchio's home, when the fox suddenly stopped and said, "Would you like to double your fortune?"

"How do you mean?"

"Would you like to multiply those five miserable gold pieces into a hundred, a thousand, two thousand times?"

"Who wouldn't! But how?"

"That's very easy. But instead of going home, you must come with us."

"And where are you going?"

"We are going to Dupeland."

Pinocchio thought for a moment, and then said resolutely, "No, I'm not going. I'm nearly at home, and I want to go to my father, who is waiting for me. Who knows how much he suffered because I didn't come home? I know I have been a very bad boy, and that the talking cricket was right when he said, 'Disobedient children never do any good in this world.' I have learnt it at my expense, for I have suffered many misfortunes! and last night, in Fire-eater's house, I was nearly . . . Oh, even to think of it, makes me shiver!"

"Well, then," said the fox, "so you really want to go home? Run along, then, and so much the worse for you!"

"So much the worse for you!" repeated the cat.

"Think well, Pinocchio, because you're losing a fortune!"

"A fortune!" repeated the cat.

"Your five gold pieces might become two thousand in one day!"   "Two thousand!" repeated the cat.

"But how could they possibly become so many?" demanded Pinocchio, opening his mouth wide in astonishment.

"I'll explain it to you right now," said the fox.

"You must know that in Dupeland there is a sacred field called the Field of Miracles. You dig a little hole in this field, and you put in it, let's say, a gold piece. Then you cover it with earth, water it from the spring with two buckets of water, sprinkle two pinches of salt over it, and go quietly to bed. During the night the gold pieces will grow and blossom; and the next morning, when you get up and go back to the field, what do you find? You find a marvellous tree, laden with as many gold pieces as an ear of corn has grains at harvest-time."

"Suppose," said Pinocchio, more bewildered than ever, "that I buried my five gold pieces in that field, how many should I find there the next morning?"

"That's very easy to tell," replied the fox. "It's a problem that can be solved on your fingers. Suppose every gold piece yields five hundred gold pieces; multiply five hundred by five, and the next morning you will find in your pocket two thousand five hundred shining gold pieces."

"Oh, wonderful!" shouted Pinocchio, dancing for joy. "When I have collected these gold pieces, I shall keep two thousand for myself, and I shall make a present of the other five hundred to both of you."

"A present – to us?" exclaimed the fox, as if offended. "God forbid!"

"God forbid!" repeated the cat.

"We do not work for gain," said the fox. "We do everything for other people."

"For other people," echoed the cat.

"What good people!" thought Pinocchio. And, instantly forgetting his father, the new coat, the primer, and all his good resolutions, he said to the fox and the cat, "Well, let's start! I shall come with you."

CHAPTER 13

The Lobster Inn

They walked, and walked, and walked, and finally towards evening, tired out, they arrived at the Lobster Inn.

"Let us stop here a little while," said the Fox, "that we may eat a bite, and rest a few hours. At midnight we must go on again, so that we can reach the Field of Miracles early tomorrow morning."

They entered the inn, and sat down at a table, but none of them had any appetite.

The poor cat had a bad indigestion, and could eat no more than thirty-five mullet with tomato sauce, and four helpings of tripe with Parmesan cheese; and, because she thought the tripe was not well seasoned, she asked three times for the butter and grated cheese.

The fox, too, would gladly have nibbled at something, but since the doctor had put him on a strict diet, he had to be content with a hare in sweet-savoury sauce, garnished with fat spring chickens and young pullets. After the hare, he ordered a special dish composed of partridges, rabbits, frogs, lizards, and other titbits, but he would not touch anything more. He said he was so

43

disgusted at the sight of food that he could not eat another mouthful.

The one who ate least of all was Pinocchio. He asked for some nuts and some bread, but he left them all on his plate. The poor child's thoughts were fixed on the Field of Miracles, and he was suffering a mental indigestion of gold pieces.

When they had supped, the fox said to their host, "Give us two nice rooms – one for Mr Pinocchio, and the other for me and my friend. We shall take a little nap before we leave. Don't forget that, at midnight, we must continue our journey."

"Yes, sir," replied the host, winking at the fox and the cat as if to say, "I understand what you are up to. We know each other."

As soon as he was in bed, Pinocchio fell asleep, and began to dream. He dreamed that he was in the middle of a field, and the field was full of small trees, the branches of which were laden with gold pieces swinging gently in the breeze, and chattering as if to say, "Whoever wants us, come and take us!" But just at the most interesting moment – that is, when Pinocchio stretched out his hand to pick a handful and put them in his pocket – he was suddenly awakened by three violent knocks on the door.

It was the innkeeper, who came to tell him that it was midnight.

"Are my companions ready?" asked Pinocchio.

"Ready! They left two hours ago."

"Why were they in such a hurry?"

"Because the cat received a message that her eldest son was very sick with chilblains, and not expected to live."

"Did they pay for our supper?"

"What an idea! They were far too well-mannered to offer such an insult to a gentleman like you."

"That's too bad! Such an insult would have been a great pleasure!" said Pinocchio, scratching his head. Then he inquired, "And where did those good friends of mine say they would wait for me?"

"In the Field of Miracles, tomorrow morning, at sunrise."

Pinocchio paid for his supper, and that of his friends, with a gold piece, and left. It was so dark that he had to grope his way, and it was impossible to see as far as his hand before his face. In the country round him, not a leaf stirred.

Only a few night birds, flying across the road from one hedge to the other, brushed Pinocchio's nose with their wings, frightening him so that he jumped back, crying, "Who goes there?"

An echo answered from the distant hills, "Who goes there? Who goes there? Who goes there?"

As he walked on he saw a little creature on the trunk of a tree, which shone with a pale faint light, like a night lamp with a china shade.

"Who are you?" asked Pinocchio.

"I am the ghost of the talking cricket," was the reply, in a low, low voice, so faint that it seemed to come from another world.

"What do you want from me?" said the marionette.

"I want to give you some advice. Go back home, and carry the four gold pieces you have left to your poor father, who is weeping and longing for you."

"Tomorrow my father will be a rich gentleman, for these four gold pieces will have become two thousand."

"My boy, never trust people who promise to make you rich in a day. They are generally crazy swindlers. Listen to me, and go back home."

"No, on the contrary I am going forward."

"It is very late."

"I am going forward."

"The night is dark."

"I am going forward."

"It's a dangerous road . . ."

"I am going forward."

"Remember that children who do as they please and want to have their own way, are sorry for it sooner or later."

"That's an old story. Good night, cricket!"

"Good night, Pinocchio. May Heaven preserve you from dangers and assassins!"

With these words, the talking cricket disappeared as suddenly as when you blow out a candle; and the path was darker than before.

45

CHAPTER 14

*Pinocchio does not listen to the good advice
of the talking cricket, and meets the assassins*

eally," said Pinocchio to himself, as he continued his journey, "how unfortunate we poor boys are! Everybody scolds us, everybody warns us, everybody advises us. When they talk you would think they are all our fathers, or our schoolmasters – all of them: even the talking cricket. Just imagine – because I would not listen to that tiresome talking cricket, who knows, according to him, how many misfortunes will befall me? I shall even meet some assassins! Fortunately I don't believe, and never have believed, in assassins. I am sure that assassins have been invented by fathers to frighten us, so that we should not dare to go out at night. But supposing I should meet them, on the road, would I be afraid of them? Certainly not! I should walk straight up to them and say, 'Mr Assassins, what do you want from me? Just remember that there's no joking with me. You had better be quiet, and go about your business!' If those wretched assassins heard me talking like that, I can just see them running away like the wind. But if, by chance, they didn't run away, I would and that would be the end of it."

Pinocchio would have continued his musings, but at that moment he thought he heard a rustling of leaves behind him.

Turning quickly, he saw two frightful black figures wrapped in charcoal sacks leaping towards him on tiptoe, like two spectres.

"There they are, for sure!" he said to himself and, not knowing where to hide his gold pieces, he put them in his mouth, under his tongue.

Then he tried to run away; but before he could take the first step, he felt himself seized by his arms, and heard two horrible, cavernous voices cry, "Your money, or your life!"

Pinocchio not being able to speak, since the money was in his mouth, made a thousand bows and gestures to show those masked fellows, whose eyes were visible only through holes in the sacks, that he was a poor puppet, and hadn't even a counterfeit farthing in his pocket.

"Come, come! Less nonsense, and hand over your money!" the two brigands cried menacingly.

But the puppet made signs with his hands, as if to say, "I haven't any!"

"Hand over your money, or you are dead!" said the taller of the assassins.

"Dead!" repeated the other.

"And after we have killed you, we shall kill your father, too!"

"Your father, too!" repeated the other.

"No, no, no, not my poor father!" cried Pinocchio in despair. But as he spoke, the gold pieces clinked in his mouth.

"Ah, ha, you rascal! So you hid your money under your tongue! Spit it out, at once!"

Pinocchio did not obey.

"Oh, so you cannot hear what we say? Wait a moment, we'll make you spit it out!"

And one of them seized the puppet by the end of his nose, and the other by his chin, and they pulled without mercy, one up, the other down, to make him open his mouth; but it was no use. Pinocchio's mouth was as tightly closed as if it had been nailed and riveted.

Then the smaller assassin drew a horrid knife, and tried to force it between his lips, like a chisel, but Pinocchio, quick as lightning, bit off his hand and spat it out. Imagine his astonishment when he saw it was a cat's paw he spat to the ground!

Encouraged by this first victory, using his nails he freed himself from the assassins and, jumping over the hedge by the roadside, fled across the country. The assassins ran after him, like dogs after a hare. The smaller one, who had lost a paw, ran on one leg, though goodness knows how he did it.

After they had run miles and miles, Pinocchio was completely exhausted. Seeing himself lost, he climbed a very tall pine-tree, and seated himself on its highest branch. The assassins tried to climb after him, but half-way up they slipped and fell to the ground, hurting their hands and feet.

Yet they did not give up. They gathered a heap of dry sticks at the foot of the tree, and set fire to it. In less than no time the pine started to burn, and blazed like a candle in the wind. Pinocchio, seeing that the flames were mounting fast, and not wanting to end his life like a roasted pigeon, leaped down from the tree-top, and ran again across the fields and vineyards. The assassins followed him, running close without seeming a bit tired.

It was nearly daybreak, and they were still running, when suddenly Pinocchio found the way barred by a wide, deep ditch full of dirty, coffee-coloured water. What was he to do?

"One, two, three!" cried the puppet and, dashing forward, he jumped over it. The assassins jumped, too; but they had not judged the distance properly, and – Swash! Splash! – they fell right in the middle of the ditch.

Pinocchio heard the splashing of water and, running, he laughed, and shouted, "A good bath to you, Mr Assassins!"

He was sure that they were drowned, when, turning to look, he saw them both running after him, still wrapped in their sacks, from which the water was dripping as if they were two leaky baskets.

CHAPTER 15

The assassins follow Pinocchio and,
having caught him, hang him
on a branch of the big oak tree

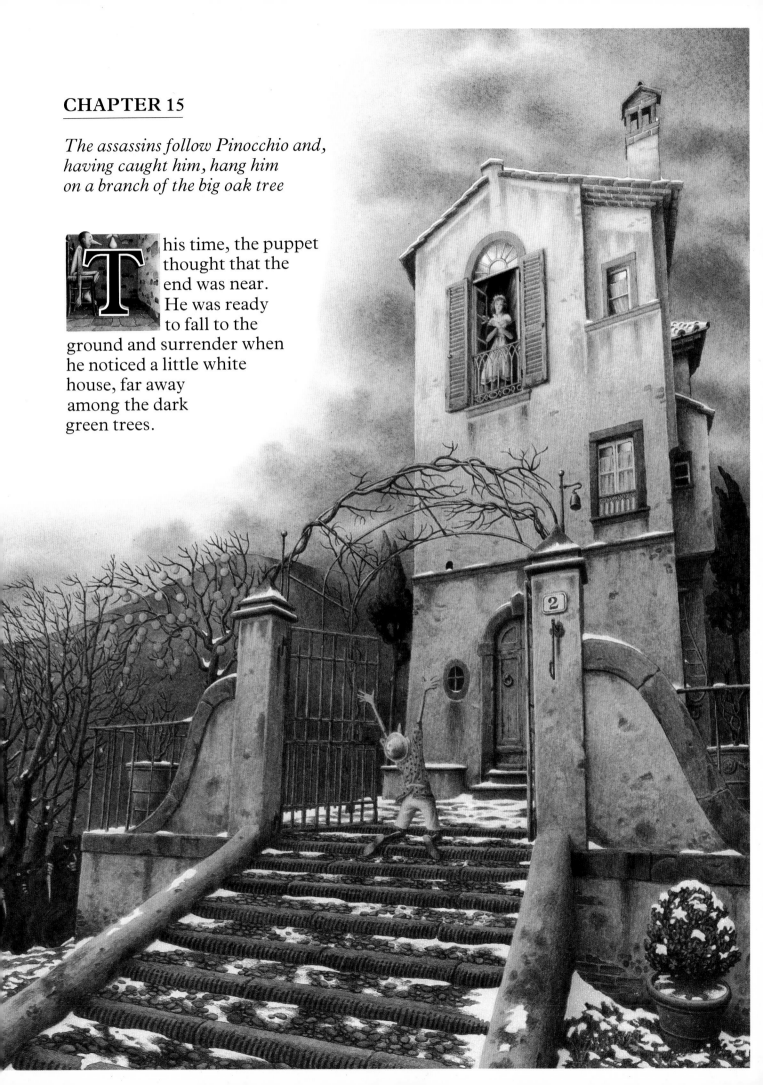

This time, the puppet thought that the end was near. He was ready to fall to the ground and surrender when he noticed a little white house, far away among the dark green trees.

"If I had enough breath to get to that house, perhaps I'd be safe," he told himself.

Wasting no time, he ran through the wood, with the assassins on his track.

After a desperate race of nearly two hours, he arrived at last, worn out, at the door of the little house.

He knocked, but no one answered. He knocked again, louder, for he heard the footsteps of the assassins; but all was silent as before.

Seeing that it was useless to knock, he began kicking the door, and beating it with his head. At that, a lovely child opened the window. Her hair was blue, and her face as white as wax; her eyes were closed, and her hands were crossed on her breast.

Without moving her lips she said in a very low voice that seemed to come from another world, "There is nobody in this house. They are all dead."

"But at least you should open the door and let me in," cried Pinocchio, weeping, and entreating her.

"I am dead, too."

"Dead? Then what are you doing at the window?"

"I am waiting for the bier to come, and take me away."

As she said this she disappeared, and the window closed itself, silently.

"Oh, beautiful blue-haired child," cried Pinocchio, "open the door, for pity's sake! Have mercy on a poor boy pursued by assass . . ."

But before he could finish, he felt himself seized by the neck, and heard those cruel threatening voices, "This time you won't escape!"

The puppet, feeling that his end was near, began to tremble, so violently that the joints of his wooden legs creaked, and the gold pieces under his tongue clinked together.

"Now, then," demanded the assassins, "will you open your mouth, or will you not? You won't answer, eh? Well, leave it to us. We'll open it for you this time!"

And, drawing two great knives as sharp as razors – Slash! they stabbed him savagely.

Luckily the puppet was made of the hardest wood, and the knives broke into a thousand pieces. Only the handles remained in the assassins' hands, who stood staring at each other.

"Now I see," said one of them, "he must be hung. Let us hang him!"

"Let us hang him!" repeated the other.

No sooner said than done. They bound his arms behind his back and, putting a running noose around his throat, they tied him to a branch of a big oak tree.

Then they sat down on the grass, and waited for his last kick; but after three hours, the puppet's eyes were still wide open, and he was kicking stronger than ever.

Losing their patience, and tired of waiting, they turned to Pinocchio, and said with a sneering voice, "Good-bye, until tomorrow, when we shall be back. And let's hope you'll be so polite as to see that we find you very dead, and your

mouth wide open!'' Then they left.

Meanwhile, a stormy north wind had begun to blow, and it raged, and whistled, and blew the poor puppet back and forth as fast as a bell-clapper on a wedding-day. It hurt him dreadfully, and the running noose tightened around his throat so that he could not breathe.

Little by little his eyes grew dim, and, although he felt that death was near, still he hoped that some kind person might come and save him. He waited and waited, but nobody came – absolutely nobody.

Then he remembered his poor father, and he stammered, half dead as he was, "O daddy! If only you were here!"

He could say no more. He closed his eyes, opened his mouth, stretched out his legs, shuddered all over, and became stiff.

CHAPTER 16

The beautiful blue-haired child saves the puppet; she puts him in bed, and calls three doctors to know whether he is alive or dead

hile poor Pinocchio, hung on a branch of the big oak tree, seemed more dead than alive, the beautiful child with blue hair looked out of the window again. She felt very sorry for the unfortunate puppet who, hanging by his neck, was dancing to the music of the cold north wind. She clapped her hands three times, faintly.

At this signal there was a rustling as of flapping wings, and a large falcon flew to the windowsill.

"What are your orders, beautiful fairy?" asked the falcon, lowering his beak in reverence – for you must know that the child with blue hair was no other than a good-hearted fairy, who had lived in that wood for more than a thousand years.

"Do you see that puppet hanging on a branch of the big oak?"

"I see him."

"Very well. Fly there quickly; break the knot that holds him, with your strong beak, and lay him gently on the grass at the foot of the tree."

The falcon flew away, and in two minutes he returned saying, "I obeyed your order."

"How did you find him?"

"He seems to be dead, but he

53

cannot be quite dead, for as soon as I loosened the running noose that strangled his neck, he murmured, 'Now I feel better!'"

The fairy clapped her hands twice, and a magnificent poodle appeared, walking upright on his hind legs, as if he were a man. The poodle was dressed like a coachman in his Sunday best. He had a three-cornered hat trimmed with gold, a white curly wig reaching his shoulders, a chocolate-coloured waistcoat with diamond buttons and two large pockets for the bones his mistress gave him at dinner, a pair of breeches of crimson velvet, silk stockings, low boots, and a kind of umbrella case, made of blue satin, to put his tail in when it was raining.

"Be quick, Medoro!" said the fairy. "Get out my finest carriage from my coach house, and drive to the wood. When you come to the big oak, you will find a poor puppet lying, half dead, on the grass. Take him up gently, put him on the cushions, and bring him to me. Do you understand?'

The poodle, to show that he understood, wagged the blue satin case he carried behind three or four times, and off he ran.

In a few minutes a beautiful carriage was driven out of the coach house. It was the colour of fresh air, and the cushions were padded with canary feathers and lined with whipped cream and custard, with sweet biscuits. It was drawn by a hundred pairs of white mice, and the poodle sitting on the box cracked his whip like a driver afraid of being late.

In less than a quarter of an hour the carriage was back again. The fairy, who was waiting at the door, took the poor puppet in her arms, carried him to a little room whose walls were mother-of-pearl, and sent at once for the most famous doctors in the neighbourhood.

The doctors came in a hurry, one after another. They were a crow, an owl, and a talking cricket.

"Gentlemen, I should like you to tell me," said the fairy, as the doctors stood around Pinocchio's bed, "I should like you gentlemen to tell me if this unfortunate puppet is dead or alive."

The crow came forward first, and felt Pinocchio's pulse; then he felt his nose, and finally his little toe. Having examined them carefully he solemnly declared, "It is my opinion that this puppet is quite dead; but if, unfortunately, he is not dead, then that would be a sure sign that he is still alive."

"I regret very much," said the owl, "to contradict the crow, my illustrious friend and colleague, but according to my opinion this puppet is still alive; but if, unfortunately, he is not alive, then that would be a sign that he is really dead."

"And have you nothing to say?" inquired the fairy, turning to the talking cricket.

"I think that when a prudent physician does not know what to say, the wisest thing he can do is to remain silent. For the rest, this puppet's face is not new to me; I have seen him before."

Pinocchio, who until that moment had seemed as lifeless as a real piece of wood, started to shudder, shaking the whole bed.

"That puppet there," continued the talking cricket, "is a perfect rogue . . ."
Pinocchio opened his eyes, but closed them again quickly.

"He is a rogue, a good-for-nothing, a vagabond . . ."
Pinocchio hid his face beneath the sheet.

"That puppet is a disobedient son, who will make his poor old father die of a broken heart!"

Just then a smothered sobbing and crying could be heard in the room. Imagine everybody's surprise when, lifting up the sheet a little, they saw that Pinocchio was crying.

"When a dead boy weeps, it's a sign that he is on the way to recovery," said the crow, solemnly.

"I am sorry to contradict my illustrious friend and colleague," said the owl, "but according to my opinion the sign indicates that he does not want to die."

CHAPTER 17

Pinocchio eats the sugar, but won't take the medicine;
however, when he sees the grave-diggers coming
to carry him away, he takes it;
then he tells a lie, and his nose grows longer
as punishment

As soon as the three doctors had left the room, the fairy came to Pinocchio. She touched his forehead with her hand, and felt that he had a dangerous fever.

Thereupon she dissolved some white powder in half a glass of water and, holding it to his lips, said lovingly, "Drink this, and in a few days you will be better."

Pinocchio looked at the glass, made a sour face, and asked in a complaining voice, "Is it sweet, or bitter?"

"It is bitter, but it will do you good."

"If it's bitter I won't drink it."

"Listen to me, and drink it!"

"I don't like anything bitter."

"If you drink it, I shall give you a lump of sugar, to take the taste out of your mouth."

"Where is the lump of sugar?"

"Here it is," said the fairy, taking one out of a golden sugar basin.

"First I want the lump of sugar, and then I'll drink the horrid bitter water."

"You promise to drink it?"

"Yes."

The fairy gave him the sugar, and Pinocchio crunched and swallowed it in a second, saying as he licked his lips, "It would be fine if sugar were medicine. I'd take it every day."

"Now keep your promise, and drink these few drops of water. They will bring back your health."

Pinocchio took the glass in his hand unwillingly. He brought it to his nose, and held it to his lips, then again to his nose, and at last he said, "It's too bitter! It's too bitter! I can't drink it!"

"How can you tell, when you haven't even tasted it!"

"Oh, I know it is! I know it from its smell. Give me another lump of sugar, and then I'll drink it."

So the fairy, with all the patience of a good mother, put another lump of sugar in his mouth, and then she offered him the glass again.

"I can't drink it like that," said the puppet, making hundreds of grimaces.

"Why can't you?"

"Because that pillow on my feet annoys me."

The fairy removed the pillow.

"It's no use. I can't drink it like that, either."

"What is the matter now?"

"The door bothers me; it's half open."

The fairy went and shut the door.

"The fact is," cried Pinocchio, bursting into tears, "I won't drink that bitter water – no, no, no . . ."

"My child, you will be sorry."

"I don't care."

"You are very ill."

"I don't care."

"This fever will send you to the other world in a few hours."

"I don't care."

"Are you not afraid to die?"

"Not a bit! I'd rather die than drink that horrid medicine!"

At that moment the door of the room opened, and four rabbits as black as ink came in, carrying a little black coffin on their shoulders.

"What do you want of me?" shouted Pinocchio, sitting up in his bed in terror.

"We have come to take you away," said the biggest rabbit.

"To take me away! But I'm not dead yet!"

"No, not quite yet, but you have only a few minutes to live, because you refused the medicine that would have made you well."

"O fairy, kind fairy," cried the puppet, "give me the glass at once; hurry, for Heaven's sake, for I don't want to die! No, I will not die!"

He took the glass in both hands, and emptied it at a draught.

"Ah, well!" said the rabbits. "This time we have made a journey for nothing." And taking the little coffin on their shoulders they left the room, murmuring and grumbling between their teeth.

A few minutes later Pinocchio jumped out of bed quite well; for you must know that wooden marionettes have the privilege of being ill very seldom and of getting well very quickly.

When the fairy saw him running and rushing about the room as gay and lively as a young rooster, she said, "So my medicine really did do you good?"

"I should say so! It brought me back to life."

"Then, for Heaven's sake, why was it so hard to make you drink it?"

"I think because we boys are all like that. We fear the medicine more than the sickness."

"Shame on you! Boys should know that the right medicine, taken in time, might save them from a serious illness, perhaps even from death."

"Oh, another time I won't make so much fuss. I'll remember those black rabbits with the coffin on their shoulders, and take the glass at once, and down it will go!"

"Now, come here, and tell me how it happened that you fell into the hands of assassins."

"It was like this: the Showman, Fire-eater, gave me some gold pieces and said, 'Here, take these to your father.' But on the road I met the fox and the cat, two very decent people, and they said, 'Would you like to change these pieces into a thousand – yes, into two thousand – gold pieces? Come with us, and we will take you to the Field of Miracles.' So I said, 'Let us go!' And they said, 'Let's stop at the Lobster Inn, and continue our way after midnight.' And when I woke up they were not there, because they had left already. Then I started after them in the dark, and I couldn't tell you how dark it was. And so I met two assassins in coal sacks, who said to me, 'Hand over your money!' And I said, 'I haven't any', because I had hidden the four gold pieces in my mouth. One of the assassins tried to put his hand in my mouth, and I bit it off; but what I spat out wasn't a hand, but a cat's paw. And the assassins ran after me, and I ran and ran until they caught me, and hung me by the neck to a tree in the wood, saying, 'We'll come back tomorrow, and then you will be dead, and your mouth will be open, and we'll get the money hidden under your tongue.'"

"Where are the four gold pieces now?" asked the fairy.

"I've lost them," answered Pinocchio. But he told a lie, for he had them in his pocket. No sooner had he told this lie than his nose, which was already very long, became two inches longer.

"Where did you lose them?"

"In the wood near by."

At this second lie, his nose became still longer.

"If you lost them near here," said the fairy, "we can search for them; for everything lost in that wood can easily be found."

"Oh! Now I remember everything," replied the puppet, greatly confused. "I didn't lose the money. I swallowed it when I was drinking your medicine."

At this third lie, his nose grew so long that poor Pinocchio could not move in any direction. If he turned one way, his nose hit the bed or the window panes; if he turned the other, it struck the walls or the door; if he raised his head a little, there was danger of putting his nose into the fairy's eyes.

The fairy looked at him, and laughed.

"What are you laughing at?" asked the puppet, much embarrassed and worried about his nose, which was growing to such a size.

"I am laughing at the lies you have told."

"How did you know I was telling lies?"

"Lies, my dear boy, can easily be recognized. There are two kinds of them: those with short legs, and those with long noses. Your kind have long noses."

Pinocchio wanted to hide his face for shame. He tried to run out of the room, but he could not, for his nose was so long that he could not go through the door.

CHAPTER 18

Pinocchio again sees the fox and the cat
and goes with them to sow his money
in the Field of Miracles

As you may imagine, the fairy let the puppet scream and cry a good half hour because of his long nose which he could not get through the door. She did this to teach him a good lesson, and to correct him of the very bad habit of lying, which is one of the worst habits a boy can have. But when she saw his face disfigured from crying, and his eyes sticking out of his head, she pitied him. So she clapped her hands, at which signal a thousand big wood-peckers flew in at the window, and perching on Pinocchio's nose, pecked away at it with so much zeal that in a few minutes the big, ridiculous thing was reduced to its usual size.

"How good you are, dear fairy," said the puppet, wiping his eyes. "I love you so much!"

"I love you too," answered the fairy, "and if you want to stay with me, you shall be my little brother, and I will be your darling sister."

"I'd like to stay with you, but what about my daddy?"

"I have thought of everything, and your father already knows everything. He will be here tonight."

"Really?" exclaimed Pinocchio, jumping for joy. "Then, dearest fairy, if you don't mind, I shall go out to meet him. I can't wait any longer to see and kiss that poor old man, who has suffered so much for me!"

"Go, by all means, but don't get lost. Take the road through the wood, and you will surely meet him."

Pinocchio left; and as soon as he reached the wood he began to run like a deer. At a certain place, in front of the big oak tree, he stopped, because he thought he heard people moving in the bushes. And indeed, there appeared all at once on the road – can you guess who? – the fox and the cat, his two travelling companions, with whom he had supped at the Lobster Inn.

"Here is our dear Pinocchio," exclaimed the fox, embracing and kissing him. "How do you come to be here?"

"How do you come to be here?" repeated the cat.

"It's a very long story," said the puppet. "I'll tell it when I have time, though you should know this much – that the other night, when you left me alone in the inn, I encountered assassins on the road."

"Assassins? Oh, my poor friend Pinocchio! And what did they want?"

"They wanted to rob me of my gold."

"Infamous people!" said the fox.

"Most infamous people!" added the cat.

"But I ran away," continued the puppet, "and they chased me until they caught me, and hung me to a branch of that oak tree." And Pinocchio pointed to the big oak.

"Did you ever hear anything more horrible!" said the fox. "What a world we are condemned to live in! Where can honest people like us find shelter?"

While talking, Pinocchio noticed that the cat was lame of her right foreleg, since the paw with all its claws was missing. So he said to her, "What has become of your paw?"

The cat wanted to say something, but got confused – so the fox answered quickly, "My friend is too modest. That is why she doesn't answer, but I shall answer for her. About an hour ago we met an old wolf on the road, who was almost fainting from hunger. He asked alms of us, but we hadn't even a fish bone to give him; so what do you think my friend did – my friend, who has the heart of a Caesar? She bit off her own paw, and gave it to the poor beast, so that he could eat something." As he told this, the fox wiped a tear.

Pinocchio was so deeply touched that he went to the cat, and whispered in her ear, "If all cats were like you, mice would be fortunate creatures!"

"And what are you doing here?" asked the fox.

"I'm waiting for my father; he might come any moment."

"And your gold pieces?"

"They are all in my pocket, except the one I spent at the inn of the Lobster."

"And to think that, by tomorrow, instead of four gold pieces they might be a thousand, or two thousand! Why not follow my advice, and bury them in the Field of Miracles?"

"Impossible, today. I'll go another time."

"Another time will be too late," said the fox.

"Why?"

"Because a rich man has bought the field, and after tomorrow nobody will be allowed to bury his money there."

"How far away is the Field of Miracles?"

"Hardly two miles. Will you come with us? You will be there in half an hour, and bury your four gold pieces at once, and after a few minutes you shall have two thousand, and return in the evening with your pockets full. Will you come?"

Pinocchio remembered the good fairy, old Geppetto, and the warnings of the talking cricket; yet in the end he did as all boys do who have no sense, and no heart – that is, he nodded his head and said to the fox and the cat, "Let's go! I'll come with you."

And off they went.

They had walked about half a day when they came to a place called Fools' Trap. As soon as they entered the city, Pinocchio saw that the streets were full of dogs who had lost their hair, and whose mouths were wide open from hunger. There were shorn sheep, trembling with cold; roosters without their crests and combs, who were begging for a grain of maize; butterflies who could not fly, because they had sold their beautiful wings; peacocks without tails, who were ashamed to be seen; and pheasants who were crawling along, mourning for their beautiful gold and silver feathers, lost for ever.

In the midst of these beggars and shame-faced beasts, from time to time elegant carriages passed by, with a fox, or a thievish magpie, or some bird of prey inside.

"But where is the Field of Miracles?" asked Pinocchio.

"Just a few yards from here."

They crossed the city and, going beyond the walls, they came to a lonely field that looked just like any other field.

"Here we are," said the fox. "Now, get to work and dig a small hole with your hands and put your gold pieces in."

Pinocchio obeyed. He dug a hole, put into it the four gold pieces he still had, and covered them up with some earth.

"Now, then," said the fox, "go to the dam close by, bring a bucket of water, and water the ground where you have sown your fortune."

Pinocchio went to the dam and, as he did not have a bucket, he took one of his old shoes, filled it with water, and watered the earth which covered his money.

"What else must I do?"

"Nothing else," answered the fox. "Now we can go away. You must come back in about twenty minutes, and you will see a little tree already growing through the earth, with its branches covered with money."

The poor puppet was beside himself with joy, and he thanked the fox and the cat a thousand times, and promised them a lovely present.

"We don't want presents," answered those two scoundrels. "It's quite enough for us to have shown you how to get rich without hard work. That makes us as happy as can be."

With these words they said good-bye to Pinocchio and, wishing him a splendid harvest, they went about their business.

CHAPTER 19

Pinocchio loses his money, and he is sent to prison
where he spends four months

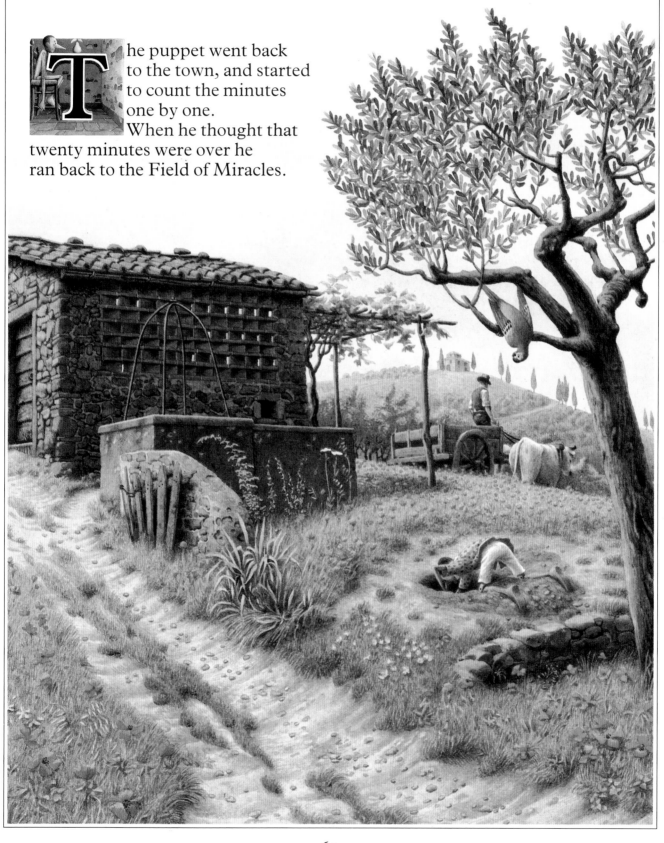

The puppet went back to the town, and started to count the minutes one by one. When he thought that twenty minutes were over he ran back to the Field of Miracles.

He ran as fast as he could, his heart beating like a grandfather clock – tick tock, tick tock – while he talked to himself.

"Suppose, instead of a thousand gold pieces, I find two thousand on the branches of the tree? Or instead of two thousand, five thousand? Or instead of five thousand, one hundred thousand? Oh, what a fine gentleman I shall be then! I shall have a magnificent palace, and a thousand wooden ponies and a thousand stables to play with, and a cellar full of lollies, and cordials, and a library brimful of candies, and tarts, and cakes, and almond biscuits, and cream puffs!"

While he was thus talking to himself, he came near the field, and stopped to look if he could see a tree, with branches laden with money; but he saw nothing. He went a little nearer – still nothing. He entered the field, went to the spot where he had buried his gold pieces, and still nothing at all. He stood there pondering; and, forgetting the rules and regulations of good manners, he took his hand out of his pocket, and scratched his head with all his might.

At that moment a loud laugh shattered the air and, looking up, he saw a large parrot sitting on a tree, cleaning the few feathers he had left.

"Why are you laughing?" asked Pinocchio angrily.

"I am laughing because while cleaning my feathers, I tickled myself under my wings."

The puppet did not answer. He went to the dam, filled his old shoe with water again, and watered the earth covering his money.

While he did so, another laugh, more impertinent than the first one, rang out over the deserted field.

"I say!" shouted Pinocchio, angrily. "May I know what you are laughing at, you ill-mannered parrot?"

"I am laughing at those simpletons who are silly enough to believe all the nonsense they hear, and who are always cheated by those who are more cunning than they are."

"Are you, perhaps, speaking of me?"

"Yes, poor Pinocchio, I am, for you are so simple as to believe that you can sow and harvest money, like beans and pumpkins. There was a time when I believed that, too, and today I am suffering for it. Today – alas, it is too late

64

— I have learnt that to earn money honestly, you must know how to do it with the labour of your hands, or with your brains."

"I don't understand," said the puppet, trembling with fear.

"Patience! I shall explain it more plainly," answered the parrot. "While you were in the city, the fox and cat returned here; they dug out your money, and ran away like the wind. You must be a quick runner if you want to catch them."

Pinocchio stood there with his mouth open, and as he did not believe what the parrot said, he began to dig up the earth he had watered. He dug, and dug, and dug, until he had a hole big enough for a haystack; but money there was none.

Then, in desperation, he ran back to the town, and went to the court house, to denounce the rascals who had robbed him.

The judge was an old gorilla, who was very very old, and looked most respectable, with his white beard and his gold spectacles without lenses, which he had to wear because of an inflammation of the eyes, that he had had for many years.

In the judge's presence, Pinocchio told all the circumstances of the infamous fraud of which he had been the victim. He gave the names, surnames, and all other details of these rascals, and finished by demanding justice.

The judge, as he was very much interested in the story, listened to him with goodwill, and was extremely sorry for him. When the puppet had told everything, he stretched out his hand and rang a bell.

At the sound, two mastiffs appeared, dressed like policemen.

The judge pointed to Pinocchio and said, "This poor fellow has been robbed of four gold pieces. Take him to the prison, immediately."

Pinocchio was flabbergasted as he heard this sentence, which came like lightning out of a blue sky. He tried to protest but the policemen did not want to waste any time, so they put their paws on his mouth, and took him to jail.

And there he remained for four months – four long months. And he would have remained longer had it not happened, fortunately, that the young Emperor of Fools' Trap, having won a big victory over his enemies, commanded a great public rejoicing. There were illuminations, fireworks, horse and bicycle races, and, first and foremost, he ordered the prisons to be opened, and every rascal to receive his freedom.

"If the others can go, I want to go too," Pinocchio told the jailer.

"Oh no, you can't," replied the jailer, "for you are not in that class."

"I beg your pardon," said Pinocchio. "I am a rascal, too."

"In that case, you are perfectly right," said the jailer, and taking off his cap respectfully, he bowed, opened the prison door, and let him out.

CHAPTER 20

*When Pinocchio is freed from the prison
he sets out for the fairy's house;
but on the way he meets a horrible serpent,
and afterwards is caught in a trap*

Imagine Pinocchio's joy when he was free again! Without losing a second he left the town, and took the road that led to the fairy's little house.

Because it had been raining incessantly, the mud was knee-deep; but Pinocchio was not discouraged. He was so eager to meet his father again, and his little blue-haired sister, that he ran and jumped like a greyhound, and the mud splashed all over him.

As he ran he said to himself, "How many dreadful things have happened to me! And I deserved them, for I am obstinate as a mule. I always wanted my own way, and never listened to those who loved me, and who had a thousand times more sense than I had. But from now I shall lead a different life, and become an obedient boy. I have learnt the lesson that disobedient children never prosper, and never gain anything. I wonder if my father is waiting for me? Shall I find him at the fairy's house? Poor daddy! It's so long since I saw him, that I can hardly wait to embrace and kiss him. Will the fairy forgive me for disobeying her? Only to think of the good care she took of me, and the kindness she showed me! If I'm alive today I owe it to her. Could anyone imagine a more ungrateful or heartless boy than I am?"

Scarcely had he finished his pondering when he stopped, suddenly frightened, and went four steps back.

What had he seen? He saw a huge serpent stretched across the road. Its skin was green, its eyes were fiery, and its pointed tail smoked like a chimney.

You cannot imagine Pinocchio's terror. He went a long way back, and sat down on a little heap of stones, waiting for the serpent to go about his business, and leave the road free.

He waited an hour; two hours; three hours; but the serpent was still there, and even from far away Pinocchio could see his glowing eyes, and the column of smoke coming from his tail.

At last Pinocchio took all his courage in both hands and, approaching the serpent, he said, in a very gentle, sweet, insinuating voice, "Excuse me, Mr Serpent, but would you be so kind as to move on one side of the road, just enough for me to pass?"

He might as well have spoken to a wall. No one answered. He began again, with that same gentle voice, "Consider, Mr Serpent, that I am going home, and my father is expecting me. It's such a long time since I have seen him! Would you let me pass on my way?"

He waited for some sign in answer to his request, but none came. On the contrary the serpent, who had until then appeared full of life, became perfectly quiet and almost rigid. He closed his eyes, and his tail stopped smoking. "Maybe he is dead," thought Pinocchio, rubbing his hands together joyfully, and, without further ado, he made to jump over him. But just as he was going to jump, the serpent rose suddenly like a spring; and the puppet, in his fright, jumped back, stumbled and fell. It was a very clumsy fall, for his head got stuck

in the mud, and his legs up in the air.

At the sight of that puppet standing on his head in the mud, and kicking with all his might, the serpent was seized with a fit of laughter; and he laughed, and laughed, and laughed, until he burst a blood vessel in his heart, and died.

And now Pinocchio started to run again as fast as he could, so as to reach the fairy's house before dark. But he got so terribly hungry that he jumped over a hedge into a field, to pick a few bunches of muscatel grapes. Would that he had not done it!

He had barely reached the vines, when – *Crack!* – his legs were caught by two sharp irons. The pain was so terrible that he saw countless stars of every hue, dancing in the sky. The poor puppet was caught in a trap put there to catch some big polecats that had been terrorizing all the poultry yards of the neighbourhood.

CHAPTER 21

Pinocchio is captured by a peasant
who makes him work as a watchdog
for his poultry yard

As you can imagine, Pinocchio began to scream and cry; but in vain, since there were no houses, and there was not a living soul to be seen on the road.

Meanwhile night came on.

Partly because of the pain caused by the trap which cut his leg, and partly because he was afraid to be alone in the dark, in the middle of the fields, Pinocchio almost fainted.

He saw a firefly above his head, and called to him, "O little firefly, won't you be so kind as to free me from this torment?"

"Poor boy!" answered the firefly, looking at him with pity. "How ever did you get caught in those sharp irons?"

"I came into the field to pick a few bunches of grapes, and . . ."

"But are they your grapes?"

"No . . ."

"And who ever taught you to take things that are not yours?"

"I was hungry . . ."

"Hunger, my child, is not a good excuse for taking what is not yours."

"That's true, that's true," said Pinocchio, "I won't do it again."

This conversation was interrupted by the sound of footsteps coming near. It was the owner of the field, coming on tiptoe to see if he had caught one of those polecats that were eating his chickens at night. When he took out his lantern from under his coat, he was astonished to see that, instead of a polecat, he had caught a boy.

"Ah, you little thief!" the peasant said, angrily. "So it's you who are eating my chickens!"

"It isn't I, it isn't I," sobbed Pinocchio. "I only came into the field to pick a few bunches of grapes!"

"He who will steal grapes will steal chickens too. Leave it to me! I'll teach you a lesson you'll remember for a while!"

He opened the trap, seized the puppet by the collar, and carried him off to his house as if he had been a lamb.

When he reached the yard in front of his house, he threw Pinocchio on the ground and, putting his foot on his neck, he said, "It's late, and I want to go to bed. I shall settle your account tomorrow. Meanwhile, as my watchdog died today you shall take his place. You shall be my watchdog."

Thereupon he put a heavy collar, covered with sharp brass knobs, on Pinocchio's neck, and fastened it so tightly that he could not slip his head through it. A long iron chain, attached to the collar, fixed it strongly to the wall.

"If it rains tonight," said the peasant, "you may go into that little kennel and lie down. You can use the straw that has served for four years as a bed for my poor dog. Remember to keep your ears pricked; and if, unluckily, thieves should come, don't forget to bark."

With this last advice, the peasant went into the house and locked the door, leaving poor Pinocchio lying in the yard, more dead than alive with cold, hunger, and fright.

From time to time he put his fingers to the collar that pinched his throat, and said, crying, "It serves me right! It serves me jolly well right! I wanted to be a good for nothing, and a vagabond. I listened to evil companions, so I have always been unlucky. If I had only been a good boy, like so many others – if I had been willing to study and to work, if I had stayed home with my poor father – I would not be here now in this lonely place, working as a watchdog for a peasant. Oh, if I could only be born again! But it's too late, now. I must have patience!"

This complaint, which came from the depth of his heart, relieved him a little. He crawled into the kennel, and fell asleep.

CHAPTER 22

Pinocchio discovers the thieves and,
as a reward for his faithfulness, is set free

He had been sleeping soundly for over two hours, when, about midnight, he was wakened by the sound of strange voices that seemed to come from the yard. He stuck the point of his nose out of his kennel, and saw four animals with dark fur, that looked like cats. They were polecats – meat-eating animals, that are especially fond of eggs and young chickens. One of them, leaving his companions, came to the door of the kennel, and said in a low tone, "Good evening, Melampo."

"My name is not Melampo," said the puppet.

"Who are you, then?"

"I am Pinocchio."

"And what are you doing there?"

"I am a watchdog."

"But where is Melampo? Where is the old dog that lived in this kennel?"

"He died this morning."

"Did he? Poor beast! He was so kind! However, judging by your looks, you seem to be a good-natured dog, too!"

"Excuse me, I am not a dog!"

"Ah! What are you, then?"

"I am a puppet."

"And you act as a watchdog?"

"Alas, I have to do it as a punishment!"

"Well, we might make the same bargain with you that we made with old

Melampo. I'm sure our conditions will satisfy you."

"And what might they be?"

"We shall come to the poultry yard one night a week, as in the past, and carry off eight chickens. We shall eat seven, and give you one, on condition, you must understand, that you pretend to be asleep when we are here, and never bark, or wake up the farmer."

"Is that what Melampo did?"

"Yes, indeed, and we always got on splendidly together. Now sleep quietly, and you can be sure we shall bring you a chicken for your breakfast, ready plucked. Do we understand each other?"

"I understand only too clearly," answered Pinocchio, shaking his head menacingly, as if saying, "We'll soon see about that!"

When the four polecats thought they were safe, they went to the poultry yard, which was near the kennel. They opened the wooden door with their teeth and claws, and slipped inside, one after the other. But, scarcely were they all inside, when the door was shut with a loud bang.

It was Pinocchio who had shut it and, to make sure, he put a big stone against it.

Then he started to bark, and he barked just like a watchdog, "Bow-wow-wow-wow!"

The peasant heard him barking, so he jumped out of bed and, taking his gun, he came to the window and called out, "What's the matter?"

"The thieves are here!" cried Pinocchio.

"Where are they?"

"In the poultry yard."

"I'm coming right away."

Quicker than you can say "Amen", the peasant had come. He went to the poultry yard, caught the four polecats and putting them into a sack he said with a pleased voice, "At last you have fallen into my hands! I could punish you, but I am not so cruel. It is enough for me if I take you to the innkeeper in the village, who will skin you and cook you in a sweet-savoury sauce, and serve you for hares. It is an honour you do not deserve, but generous people like me are ready to do a good service."

Then he went to Pinocchio, caressed him and, among other questions, he asked him, "How did you discover these thieves? To think that Melampo, my faithful Melampo, never could find anything!"

The puppet could have told the truth – that is, he could have told the peasant of the shameful agreement between the dog and the polecats – but he remembered that the dog was dead, and he said to himself, "What good will it do if I accuse the dead? A dead person is dead and gone. The best thing to do is to leave him in peace."

"Were you awake, or asleep, when these rascals arrived?" asked the peasant.

"I was asleep," answered Pinocchio, "but they woke me by talking loudly, and one of them even came to my kennel, and said, 'If you promise not to bark, or wake up the peasant, we shall give you a nicely plucked chicken.' Imagine the impudence, offering such a proposition! I may be a puppet, and I may be full of faults, but I would never go with thieves, nor take a share in stolen goods!"

"Good for you, my boy!" said the peasant, patting him on the shoulder. "Such sentiments do credit to you. And to show how grateful I am, I give you back your freedom, that you may go home." And he took off the dog's collar.

CHAPTER 23

*Pinocchio weeps for the death of the beautiful blue-haired child;
then he meets a pigeon who carries him to the seashore, where he
dives into the water to save his father*

When Pinocchio was freed from that heavy, humiliating collar on his neck, he started out across the fields, never stopping for a second until he reached the road which led to the fairy's house.

When he reached it, he stopped to look down on the country-side. He could see plainly, with his naked eye, the site where he unluckily met the fox and the cat. He could see the wood with the big oak on which he had been hanged; but, although he looked everywhere, he could not see the little house where the lovely blue-haired child had lived.

Driven by a sad foreboding, he ran with all his might and in a few minutes he reached the field where the little white house had once stood. But the little white house was no longer there. Instead there was a little piece of white marble on which these sad words were engraved:

HERE LIES

THE BLUE-HAIRED CHILD

WHO DIED OF SORROW

ON BEING DESERTED BY HER

LITTLE BROTHER

PINOCCHIO

I leave you to imagine the puppet's feelings when he had spelt out this inscription. He fell to the ground and, kissing the cold stone a thousand times, burst into a flood of tears. He cried all night, and at dawn he was still crying, although he had no more tears. His wailing and moaning were so loud and penetrating that they were echoed from all the neighbouring hills.

As he wept he said, "O dear fairy, why are you dead? Why didn't I die – I who am so wicked – instead of you, who were so good? And my father, where is he? O dear little fairy, tell me where I can find him, for I want to stay with him for ever, and never, never leave him. Dear fairy, tell me it is not true that you are dead! If you really love me, if you love your little brother, come to life just once more; come back as you were before! Are you not sorry to see me here alone, abandoned by everybody? Should the assassins come again, they will hang me, and then I shall be dead for ever. What can I do, alone in the world? Now that I have lost you, and my father, who will look after me? Where shall I sleep? Who will make me a new jacket? Oh, it will be better, a hundred times better, if I die too! Yes, I want to die! Boo-hoo-hoo!'' In this desperate state he tried to tear his hair, but as it was made of wood, he could not even stick his fingers through it.

At this moment a large pigeon, flying high above him, stopped with outstretched wings, and called to him, "Tell me, child, what are you doing down there?"

"Don't you see? I'm crying!" said Pinocchio, looking towards the voice, and rubbing his eyes with his jacket.

"Tell me," continued the pigeon, "do you know, among your friends, a puppet called Pinocchio?"

"Pinocchio? Did you say Pinocchio?" shouted the puppet, jumping to his feet. "I'm Pinocchio!"

At this answer, the pigeon quickly alighted to the ground. He was larger than a turkey. "Do you know Geppetto, too?" he asked.

"Do I know him? He is my poor father! Has he spoken to you of me? Will you take me to him? Is he still alive? Tell me quickly, for Heaven's sake, is he still alive?"

"I left him three days ago on the sea coast."

"What was he doing?"

"He was making a little boat to cross the ocean in. The poor man has been wandering around the world more than three months, and looking for you. As he couldn't find you, he decided to search for you in distant countries."

"How far is it from here to the sea coast?" Pinocchio asked anxiously.

"Nearly six hundred miles."

"Nearly six hundred miles? O dear pigeon, what a fine thing it would be if I had wings like you."

"If you want to go, I shall carry you."

"How?"

"Astride on my back. Are you very heavy?"

"Heavy? No, indeed! I'm as light as a feather."

Without wasting another word, Pinocchio jumped on the pigeon's back, with a leg on each side of him like a rider on a horse, and shouted gaily, "Gallop, gallop, little horse, for I'm in a terrible hurry!"

The pigeon took flight, and in a few minutes he was so high that they almost touched the clouds. Once at that great height, the puppet grew very curious, and looked down; but he got so frightened, and the sight made him so dizzy, that he put his arms tight around the neck of his feathered steed to save himself from falling off. They flew all day.

Towards evening, the pigeon said, "I am so thirsty!"

"And I am so hungry!" added Pinocchio.

"Let us stop a few minutes at this dovecote; then we shall continue our flight, and by dawn we shall be at the sea coast."

They entered a deserted dovecote, where there was nothing but a basin of water, and a basket full of green seed.

The puppet had never in his life been able to eat green seed, for, as he said, it turned his stomach; but that evening he could not eat enough of it, and when the basket was empty he said to the pigeon, "I couldn't have believed green seed could taste so good!"

"You will learn, my lad," replied the pigeon, "that when you are really hungry, and there is nothing else to eat, even green seed becomes delicious. Hunger is the best cook."

After having finished this little meal they did not rest, but continued their journey. The next morning they arrived at the seashore.

The pigeon stopped to let Pinocchio dismount, and then quickly flew away. He did not want to be thanked for having done a good deed.

The beach was full of people, who were shouting and gesticulating as they looked out to the sea.

"What's happened?" Pinocchio asked of an old woman.

"A poor father has lost his son, and he intends crossing the sea in a small boat, to search for him; but the waves are so high that the boat will capsize."

"Where is the boat?"

"Right there, where my finger points," said the old woman, pointing to a little boat which, at that distance, looked like a nutshell with a very small man in it.

Pinocchio looked closely, and uttered a piercing cry, "It's my father! It's my father!"

Meanwhile the little boat, thrown by the angry waves, once disappeared completely, then re-appeared on the top of a wave. Pinocchio, standing on a high rock, called his father by name, again and again, signalling with his hands, with his cap, and with his handkerchief.

Although Geppetto was very far away, he seemed to recognize his son, for he waved with his cap, and he also made signs as if he would like to return to land; but the sea was so furious that he could not use his oars.

Suddenly there came a huge wave, and the little boat disappeared. They waited to see it again.

"Poor man!" said the fishermen, who were standing together on the beach. And murmuring a prayer they turned to go home.

Suddenly they heard a desperate shout and looking back, they saw a boy jumping into the sea from a rock, crying, "I will save my father!"

Pinocchio, being made of wood, floated easily, and swam like a fish. They saw him disappear under the water, beaten about by the waves, and then he reappeared. In the distance, now a leg appeared, now an arm, but at last they lost sight of him altogether.

"Poor boy!" said the fishermen on the beach; and, murmuring a prayer, they went home.

CHAPTER 24

Pinocchio arrives at Busy Bee Island
and finds the fairy again

oping to arrive in time to save his poor father, Pinocchio swam all night.

And what a terrible night it was! The rain came down like a flood, with hailstones and terrible thunderclaps, while flashes of lightning made the world as bright as day.

Towards morning, he saw in the distance a long strip of land. It was an island in the midst of the sea.

He tried in vain to reach the shore, the tumbling waves tossed him everywhere, as if he were straw or a stick. At last, happily, there came a huge wave that carried him out and threw him violently on the shore. He struck the shore with such force that all his ribs and joints rattled; but he comforted himself by saying, "That was another miraculous escape!"

Slowly, slowly the clouds cleared, the sun came out in all his splendour, and the sea became as quiet and smooth as oil.

The puppet spread his clothes to dry in the sun, and began looking in every direction over that huge expanse of water to see if there was a small boat anywhere with a small man in it. But although he looked and looked, he saw only the sky and the sea, and the sails of some ships; but they were so far away that they looked no bigger than flies.

"I wish I knew the name of this island!" he said. "If only I could know that decent people lived here, who do not hang boys on trees! But is there nobody I can ask all these questions?"

The idea of being alone, all alone in a country where nobody lived, made him so melancholy that he was just about to cry when he saw a big fish near the shore, swimming by. It was quietly going about its own business with its head out of water. Since he did not know its name, he cried loudly, "Hullo, Mr Fish. May I have a word with you?"

"Even two, if you like," answered the fish, who was a dolphin, but so polite that there were few like him in the seas of the world.

"Would you be so kind as to tell me if there are inhabited places on this island, where one may eat without fear of being eaten?"

"Certainly there are," answered the dolphin. "There is one not very far from here."

"Which road will lead me there?"

"Take the path on your left, and follow your nose. You can't make a mistake."

"Tell me something else. You swim in the sea all day and all night. Have you, by chance, seen a small boat with my father in it?"

"Who is your father?"

"He is the best father in the world; and I am very likely the worst son."

"As we had a very bad storm last night," said the dolphin, "the boat was probably sunk."

"And my father?"

"By this time he must have been eaten by the huge shark that has been spreading death and misery in these waters for a long time."

"Is he very big, this shark?" asked Pinocchio, frightened and trembling.

"Is he big?" asked the dolphin. "Well, just to give you an idea, I shall merely tell you that he is larger than a five-storey house, and his mouth is so wide and deep that it would easily hold a railway train, with its engine smoking and all."

"Heavens above!" cried the terrified puppet and, dressing quickly, he turned to the dolphin saying, "Good-bye, Mr Fish, excuse the trouble I have caused you, and many thanks for your kindness."

Then he hurried down the little path, almost running. At the least noise he looked behind him, fearing to see that horrible shark as large as a five-storey house, and with a railway train in his mouth, pursuing him.

He had travelled about half an hour when he came to Busy Bee town. On the streets people were hurrying back and forth, on business. Everybody had something to do; everybody was working; you could not have found an idler or a tramp if you had searched with a lamp.

"I see," lazy Pinocchio told himself, "that this place will never do for me. I was not born for work."

By this time he was terribly hungry, for he had had nothing to eat for more than twenty-four hours, not even a dish of green seed.

What could he do? To get some food, there were only two ways: ask for work, or beg for pennies or bread.

He was ashamed to beg. His father had told him several times that only the aged and the crippled have a right to beg. Poor, really poor in this world – those who really deserve help and pity – are those who, by reason of old age or sickness, are no longer able to earn their living by their own labour. It is everybody else's duty to work; and if they refuse to work, and are hungry, so much the worse for them.

Just at that moment a man passed by, tired and panting. He was pulling, with great difficulty, two carts loaded with charcoal.

Pinocchio judged, by his look, that he was a kind man; so he approached him and, casting his eyes downward in shame, he said in a low tone, "Will you please give me a penny, for I am dying of hunger."

"Not only one penny," answered the man, "but I shall give you two, if you'll help me draw home these loads of charcoal."

"I am surprised at you!" answered Pinocchio, offended. "Let me tell you that I am not a donkey! I do not draw carts."

"That's all right!" the coal dealer answered. "But then, my boy, if you are really so hungry, eat a couple of slices of your pride, and take care you don't get indigestion!"

A few minutes later a mason passed by, carrying a load of lime on his shoulder.

"Sir, would you be so kind as to give a penny to a poor boy who is hungry?"

"With pleasure. Come with me and carry lime," answered the bricklayer, "and instead of one penny, I shall give you five."

"But lime is so heavy," objected Pinocchio, "and I don't want to get tired."

"If you don't want to get tired, my boy, amuse yourself with being hungry, and much good may it do you!"

In less than half an hour twenty people passed by, and Pinocchio begged of all of them, but they all answered, "Are you not ashamed? Instead of begging on the road, go to work, and earn your living!"

At last a kind little woman appeared carrying two pails of water.

"Kind lady, will you let me have a drink of water from your pail?" asked Pinocchio, who was burning with thirst.

"Yes, drink, my child," said the little woman, putting the pails down.

When Pinocchio had had a good drink, he wiped his mouth, and said, "Now I'm thirsty no more. If only I were no longer hungry!"

The good woman, hearing these

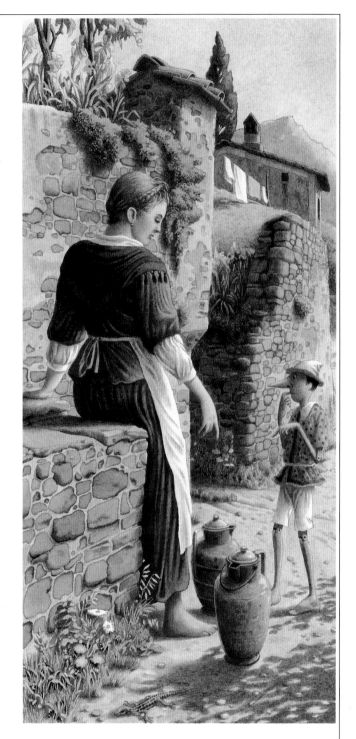

words, said quickly, "If you carry one of these pails home, I'll give you a big piece of bread."

Pinocchio looked at the pail, and said neither yes nor no.

"And with the bread, I shall give you a nice dish of cauliflower, with oil and vinegar," added the good woman.

Pinocchio looked at the pail again, but he did not say yes or no.

"And after cauliflower, I shall give you some tasty sweets."

This last temptation Pinocchio could not resist; and he said resolutely, "All right, then! I will carry the pail home for you."

The pail was very heavy, and, his hands not being strong enough to hold it, the puppet had to put it on his head.

When they arrived home, the good woman led Pinocchio to a little table already set, and put the bread, the cauliflower, and the sweets before him.

Pinocchio did not eat like a human being: he gobbled everything. His stomach was like a tenement house that had been uninhabited for five months.

Bite by bite his hunger was appeased, and he raised his head to thank his benefactress. Immediately he looked at her he uttered a long "O-o-o-oh!" of astonishment, and sat there with his fork in the air, his mouth full of bread and cauliflower, his eyes wide open as if he had been bewitched.

"What is the matter with you?" asked the good woman, laughing.

"Because, it's . . ." stammered Pinocchio, "it's . . . it's . . . you are like . . . you remind me of . . . Yes, yes, yes. The same voice . . . the same eyes . . . the same hair . . . You have blue hair, too, just as she had! O dear fairy, O dear fairy, tell me, is it you? Is it really you? Don't make me cry any more! If you only knew! I have cried so much, I have suffered so much!"

As he said this, Pinocchio fell on his knees before her, and threw his arms round that mysterious little woman, and began to cry bitterly.

CHAPTER 25

Pinocchio promises the fairy to be good and study,
because he is tired of being a puppet
and wishes to become a really good boy

At first the little woman would not admit that she was the blue-haired fairy, but seeing that she had been found out, and not wishing to continue the comedy any longer, she acknowledged the fact, saying to Pinocchio, "You rascal of a puppet, how did you recognize me?"

"It was my love for you that told me."

"Do you remember? When you left me I was a little girl, and now I am a woman, nearly old enough to be your mother."

"I like that very much, because instead of calling you little sister, I shall call you mother. I've always wanted to have a mother, as other boys. But how did you manage to grow so quickly?"

"That's a secret."

"Teach it me! I would like to be a little bigger. Look at me! I've never been more than a Tom Thumb."

"But you can't grow," answered the fairy.

"Why not?"

"Because puppets never grow. They are born puppets, they live puppets and they die puppets."

"I'm sick of always being a puppet!" cried Pinocchio, slapping his wooden head. "It's about time I became a man, like other people!"

"If you only deserved it, you could become one."

"Really? And what can I do to deserve to become a man?"

"It's very easy: you begin by being a good boy."

"Why? Do you mean to say that I'm not a good boy?"

"You are anything but! Good boys are obedient, and you . . ."

"I am never obedient."

"Good boys like to work and study, and you . . ."

"And I am an idle vagrant all the year round."

"Good boys always tell the truth . . ."

"And I always tell lies."

"Good boys like to go to school . . ."

"And school gives me a pain. But from this day forward, I shall turn over a new leaf."

"Do you promise to do that?"

"Yes, I do. I shall be a good little boy, and be the consolation of my father. Where can my poor father be?"

"I don't know."

"Will I ever be lucky enough to see him again?"

"I hope so. Yes, I am sure of it."

Hearing this, Pinocchio was so happy that he took the fairy's hands and kissed them, almost mad with joy. Then, looking up at her with loving eyes, he said, "Tell me, mother dear, it wasn't true, then, that you were dead?"

"It seems not," answered the fairy, smiling.

"If you only knew how sad I was and how my heart ached, when I read: 'HERE LIES ...'!"

"I know, and that is why I have forgiven you. As you were really sorry, I knew that you had a good heart; and if a child has a good heart, even if he is mischievous and full of bad habits, there is hope that he will mend his ways. That is why I came here to look for you. I shall be your mamma ..."

"Oh, lovely!" shouted Pinocchio, jumping for joy.

"You must always obey me, and do as you are told."

"Oh yes, yes, yes!"

"Tomorrow," added the fairy, "you will start to go to school."

Pinocchio grew a little less joyful.

"Then you will choose some profession or trade, whichever you would like ..."

Pinocchio made a wry face.

"What are you muttering between your teeth?" asked the fairy, angrily.

"I was saying," grumbled Pinocchio, "that it seems to me too late for me to go to school now."

"No, my lad! Remember always that it's never too late to learn and get educated."

"But *I* don't want to learn any profession or trade . . ."

"Why not?"

"Because I don't like work."

"My child," said the fairy, "people who talk like that generally end in a hospital, or in a prison. Remember that every man, rich or poor, must find something to do in this world; everybody must work. Woe to those who lead idle lives! Idleness is a dreadful disease, of which one should be cured immediately in childhood; if not, one never gets over it."

These words touched Pinocchio's heart. He lifted his head quickly, and said to the fairy, "I will study, I will work. I will do everything you tell me, for I am sick of being a puppet. I want to become a real boy, whatever I have to do for it. You promised that I could, didn't you!"

"Yes, it's true, I promised, and now it depends on you."

CHAPTER 26

Pinocchio and his schoolmates
go to the seashore to see the terrible shark

Next day Pinocchio went to school. Imagine what those mischievous boys did when they saw a puppet coming to their school! It seemed as if their laughter would never come to an end. One took his cap away, another pulled his jacket behind. One of the boys tried to make a big moustache under his nose with ink, and another again tried to tie strings to his hands and feet, to make him dance.

Pinocchio pretended not to notice them at first; but at last he lost his patience and, turning to his worst teasers, he told them menacingly, "Take care, boys! I didn't come here to be your clown! I respect others, and I want to be respected."

"Good for you, peacock! You talk like a book!" howled the rogues, laughing more than ever; and one of them, more impertinent than the others, put out his hand to seize the puppet's nose.

But he was not quick enough, for Pinocchio kicked his shins under the table.

"Oh! Oh! What hard feet!" cried the boy, rubbing the bruises on his aching shins.

"And what elbows! They're even harder than his feet!" exclaimed another, who had received a blow in the stomach for his rude jokes.

After a few kicks and blows, Pinocchio won the respect and liking of the whole school, and they all made friends with him.

Even the master praised him, because he was attentive, studious, and intelligent, first to arrive at school, and the last to leave when school was over.

His only fault was that he made too many friends. Some of these friends were well known as good-for-nothings, unwilling to study. The master warned him daily, and the good fairy never failed to repeat it.

"Be careful, Pinocchio! Those bad friends of yours will end up by making you lose your love for your books. I hope they won't lead you into any great trouble."

"Oh, there's no such danger!" answered the puppet, shrugging his shoulders, and touching his forehead with his finger as if to say, "There's too much good sense here inside!"

Now, it happened one day, as he was on his way to school, that he met some of these friends, who asked him, "Have you heard the great news?"

"No."

"They say that, not far away from here, there's a shark in the sea as big as a mountain."

"You don't say so! I wonder if it's the same shark that was there on the night when my poor father was drowned?"

"We're going to the beach to see it. Will you come too?"

"Not I! I'm going to school."

"Why should you go to school? We can go to school tomorrow. One lesson more or less won't change us, we'll still remain the same blockheads."

"But what will the master say?"

"He can say what he likes. He is paid to find fault all day long."

"And my mother?"

"Oh, mothers never find out anything," answered those wicked boys.

"I know what I'll do," said Pinocchio. "I have certain reasons for seeing the shark, but I'll go after school."

"You poor blockhead!" said one of them. "Do you think a fish of that size will wait for you? When he's tired of being in one place, he'll go to another, and then that'll be that!"

"How long does it take to go to the beach?" asked the puppet.

"We can be there and back in an hour."

"Well, come on then! Whoever runs fastest is the best chap!" cried

Pinocchio.

At this starting sign, all the boys ran across the fields, with their books and slates under their arms. Pinocchio led them, for he ran as if he had wings on his feet.

From time to time he turned to poke fun at his friends, who were a long way behind him; and when he saw them panting, covered with dust, and with their tongues hanging out, he laughed heartily. The poor boy did not guess at that moment what terrors and dreadful disasters were awaiting him.

CHAPTER 27

*Great battle between Pinocchio and his friends, during which
one of them is wounded and Pinocchio is arrested*

hen he arrived at the shore, Pinocchio looked at the sea, but he saw no shark. The sea was as smooth as a great mirror.

"Well, where's the shark?" he asked, turning to his friends.

"Perhaps he has gone to breakfast," said one of them, laughing.

"Or perhaps he went to bed to have a nap," said another, laughing still louder.

Their silly answers and stupid laughter told Pinocchio that it was all a joke, and that he had believed a lie. He was very angry, and he said indignantly, "May I know what your idea was in telling me that story about the shark?"

"It was great fun, to be sure!" the rogues answered in chorus.

"Well, what was it?"

"We wanted you to stay away from school, and come with us. Aren't you ashamed to be so proper and industrious every day? Aren't you ashamed to study so hard?"

"And why should you mind how hard I study?"

"We mind it because you make us look so small in the master's eyes."

"Why?"

"Because boys who study always make those who don't small by comparison, and we don't like it. We have some pride, too."

"What can I do, then, to please you?"

"You must do as we do, and hate the school, and the lessons, and the master – our three great enemies."

"And suppose I choose to keep on studying?"

"Then we'll have nothing to do with you, and we'll take the very first chance to get even with you!"

"Really, you make me laugh," said the puppet, shaking his head.

"Take care, Pinocchio," said one of the big boys, facing him. "Don't think you can lord it over us! Don't think you can crow over us! If you aren't afraid of us, we're not afraid of you. Remember you're alone, and we are seven."

"Seven, like the seven deadly sins," said Pinocchio laughing.

"Did you hear that? He has insulted us. He has called us the seven deadly sins!"

"Pinocchio, say you're sorry, or it will be the worse for you!"

"Coo-coo!" said the puppet, putting his outstretched fingers to his nose.

"Pinocchio, you'll be sorry!"

"Coo-coo!"

"We'll beat you like a donkey!"

"Coo-coo!"

"You'll go home with a broken nose!"

"Coo-coo!"

"I'll give you 'Coo-coo'!" shouted the most daring of the boys. "Take this for a start, and keep it for supper!" With this, he gave him a blow on the head.

But it was, as the saying goes, give and take, for the puppet, as was to be expected, returned the blow, and in a moment the fight became general and furious.

Pinocchio was alone, but he defended himself like a hero. His hard wooden feet kept his enemies at a respectful distance. Wherever those feet touched, they left a black mark that would not easily be forgotten.

The bad boys, angry because they could not get near Pinocchio, began to use other weapons. They unstrapped their school bags, and began to throw their books, primers and grammars, dictionaries, geography and other school books. But the puppet had sharp eyes, and dodged so quickly, that the books all flew over his head into the sea.

What do you suppose the fish did? Thinking those books were something to eat, they came in shoals; but hardly had they tasted a page or two, or a cover page, when they spat it out again, with a grimace that seemed to say, "We are used to much better food than this!"

The fight was growing more furious when suddenly a big crab that had come out of the water and climbed on to the beach called loudly, in a voice like a trumpet with a cold, "Stop it, you rascals! These schoolboy fights always end badly. Something bad will surely happen!"

Poor crab! He might as well have preached to the wind. Pinocchio was no better than the rest, and said rudely to him, "Shut up, you detestable crab! Take rather some lozenges for the cold in your throat! Go to bed, and take some medicine!"

Just then the boys, who had thrown away all their own books, saw Pinocchio's school bag lying on the ground, and in less time than it takes to tell it they took possession of it.

Among the books there was a large one bound in strong board, with leather back and corners. It was a Treatise on Arithmetic. You can imagine for yourselves how heavy and large it must have been!

One of these rascals seized the volume, and threw it at Pinocchio's head, with all the force he could muster. But, instead of hitting the puppet, it struck one of his own friends on the head.

The child turned as white as a sheet, and shouted, "Oh, mamma, help me! I am dying!" And fell his full length on the sand.

At that, the frightened boys ran away, and soon they were out of sight.

But Pinocchio stayed there, and although from sorrow and fright he was more dead than alive, he wet his handkerchief in the sea, and put it on the poor boy's temples, weeping bitterly, calling him by name, and saying, "Eugene! Poor Eugene! Open your eyes and look at me! Why don't you answer? I didn't hurt you! Believe me, it wasn't I! Open your eyes, Eugene. If you keep them shut, I shall die too. Alas! Alas! What shall I do? How shall I have the courage to go back to my mother? What will become of me? Where can I fly to hide myself? Oh, how many thousand times better would it have been if I had gone to school! Why did I listen to bad friends? They are my ruin! The master told me so, and my mother said, 'Beware of evil companions!' But I am obstinate . . . and a fool. I listen to them . . . and then do as I please! And afterwards, I have to suffer for it. It has always been so since I was born. I've never had a really good quarter of an hour in my life. Oh dear, oh dear, what will become of me?"

Pinocchio was still crying, moaning, and striking his head, and calling to Eugene, when suddenly he heard approaching footsteps. He turned, and saw two policemen.

"What are you doing there on the ground?" they asked the puppet.

"I am helping my schoolmate."

"Is anything wrong with him?"

"I think so."

"No doubt about it!" said one of the policemen, bending over Eugene, and looking at him closely. "This boy is wounded on the temple. Who did it?"

"Not I," stammered Pinocchio, frightened.

"If it wasn't you, who was it then?"

"Not I," repeated Pinocchio.

"What was he wounded with?"

"With this book."

The puppet picked up the Treatise on Arithmetic, bound in board and leather, and showed it to the policeman.

"And whose book is this?"

"Mine."

"That's enough; there's no more to say. Get up, and come with us!"

"But I . . ."

"Come along!"

"But I am innocent . . ."

"Come along!"

Before leaving, the policemen called some fishermen who were rowing near the shore, and said to them, "We are leaving this wounded boy with you. Take him home and look after him. We shall be back tomorrow."

Then they turned to Pinocchio, who had to walk between them, and they said as a military command, "Forward! And step lively, or it will be much the worse for you!"

Without waiting for them to repeat it, the puppet set out on the path that led to the village. The poor puppet did not know where his head was, but thought he was dreaming a dreadful dream. He was almost beside himself. His eyes saw double, his legs trembled, his tongue stuck to the roof of his mouth, so that he could not speak. Yet in the midst of his awe and bewilderment there was one thought that pierced his tormented heart like a thorn; the thought that he would have to pass under the good fairy's windows between two policemen. He would rather have died.

They had just entered the village when the wind blew off Pinocchio's cap, and carried it some ten yards away.

"Do you mind if I go and get my cap?" Pinocchio asked the policeman.

"Yes, go, but hurry."

The puppet picked up his cap, but instead of putting it on his head, he took it between his teeth, and began running towards the sea.

Thinking it would be hard to catch him, the policeman sent a big mastiff after him, that had won the first prizes in all the dog races. Pinocchio ran, but the dog ran faster. People all came to the windows, or ran down the street, to see the end of that fierce race. But they could not see it, for Pinocchio and the dog raised so much dust on the street that in a few minutes nothing could be seen.

CHAPTER 28

Pinocchio is in danger of being fried as a fish

There was a moment during this fierce race when Pinocchio felt himself lost; for you must know that Alidoro – that was the mastiff's name – had almost caught him.

The puppet could hear the dreadful beast panting close behind him; they were separated only by inches, and he even felt its hot breath.

Fortunately, by this time, he was near the beach, and it was only a few steps to the sea.

As soon as he reached the shore the puppet jumped, like a frog, and he was far out in the water. Alidoro wanted to stop, but as he was going so fast he was carried out into the water, too. Unfortunately he could not swim, so he pawed desperately, trying to keep his nose above water; but the more he tried, the more he went under.

When he rose to the surface his eyes were almost jumping out of his head, and he barked, "I'm drowning! I'm drowning!"

"Drown, then!" answered Pinocchio, who was now a good distance away, and out of all danger.

"Help me, Pinocchio! Save my life! Oh! Oh!"

At that desperate cry the puppet, who was really very kind-hearted, took pity on him and, turning to the dog, he said, "If I save your life, do you promise not to bother me any more, or run after me?"

"I promise! I promise! Be quick, for pity's sake, for in another half-minute I'll be dead!"

Pinocchio still hesitated, but then he remembered his father's saying that no one ever loses by doing a good deed. He swam to Alidoro and holding him by the tail with both hands, he pulled him safe and sound to the dry sandy beach.

The poor dog could not stand up. He had drunk, in spite of himself, so much salt water that he was like a balloon. However, the puppet did not dare to trust him completely, so he thought it better to jump into the sea again.

As he swam away he called to the friend he had rescued, "Good-bye, Alidoro! A good journey to you, and give my love at home."

"Good-bye, Pinocchio!" answered the dog. "A thousand thanks for saving my life. You were very kind to me, and in this world one good deed deserves another. Should you ever need me, I shall remember you."

Pinocchio went on swimming, keeping near the shore. At last, he thought he had reached a safe place. Looking round the beach, he saw a cave among the rocks, with a long column of smoke coming out of it.

"There must be a fire in that cave," he said to himself. "So much the better! I can warm and dry myself, and then? And then we shall see."

Having come to this decision, he swam near the rocks. But just as he was climbing out, he felt something rising under the water, and it lifted him out on the beach. He tried to escape, but it was too late, for, to his great surprise, he found himself in a big net, among a huge number of fish of every shape and size, flapping and jumping as if they were all mad.

At the same time he saw, coming out of the cave, a fisherman who was so ugly that he looked like a sea monster. On his head there grew thick green tufts, like grass. His skin was green, his eyes were green, and his long beard that reached to the ground was green. He looked like a huge green lizard, standing on his hind legs.

When the fisherman had taken the net out of the sea, he shouted joyfully, "Thank Heaven! I shall have a fine meal of fish today!"

"How lucky I am not to be a fish," said Pinocchio to himself, having gathered a little courage.

The net full of fish was taken into the cave, which was dark and smoky and in the middle of it there was a big frying-pan full of boiling oil, which smelled so strongly that it nearly took one's breath away.

"Now we shall see the fish we've caught!" said the green fisherman, and, putting one of his big, misshapen hands, which looked like bakers' shovels, into the net, he took out a handful of mullet.

"These mullet will be good!" he said, looking at them, and smelling them with anticipation. Then he threw them into a pan without any water.

He repeated this operation several times; and, as he drew out the fish, his mouth watered, and he said joyfully, "These whiting will be excellent! ... These sardines are exquisite! ... These crabs will be excellent! ... These anchovies will be fine!"

As you may imagine, the whiting, the sardines, the crabs, and the anchovies all went together into the dish, to keep the mullet company.

The last in the net was Pinocchio.

When the fisherman pulled him out, he opened wide his green eyes, and cried, almost frightened, "What kind of fish is this? I have never tasted such a fish!"

Having looked him over carefully several times, he finished by saying, "I see: it must be a crab."

Pinocchio was hurt at being mistaken for a crab, and he said indignantly, "What do you mean by calling me a crab? Nice way to treat me! Let me tell you, I'm a puppet."

"A puppet?" said the fisherman. "In truth, a puppet fish is new to me. All the better! I shall eat you with very great pleasure!"

"Eat me? Will you understand once for all that I am not a fish? Don't you see that I can talk and reason as you do?"

"That's right," answered the fisherman. "And now, seeing you are a fish that can speak and reason as I do, I shall treat you with the greatest consideration."

"And what will that be?"

"As a token of friendship, and particular consideration, I shall let you choose how you should be cooked. Would you prefer to be fried in oil in a pan, or stewed with tomato sauce?"

"To tell the truth," answered Pinocchio, "if I must choose, I'd prefer to get back my freedom, and go home."

"You're joking! How can you think I'd lose this chance to taste such a rare fish? You don't catch puppet fish every day. Leave it to me: I shall fry you in the pan with all the other fish, and you'll be quite happy. To be fried in company is always a consolation."

Hearing this, the miserable Pinocchio cried and screamed, and begged for mercy, sobbing, "How much better it would have been if I had gone to school! I pay dearly for listening to such friends! OH! Oh! Oh!" And because he wriggled like an eel, and made every effort to escape from the green fisherman's hands, the fisherman took a long bulrush and, binding him hand and foot like a sausage, threw him into the dish with the others.

Then he got a wooden jar full of flour, and began rolling all the fish in it; and as fast as he was done with them, he threw them into the frying-pan.

The first to dance in the boiling oil were the poor whiting; then came the crabs, the sardines, the sole, and the anchovies. At last it was Pinocchio's turn, who, being so near death – and such a terrible death – trembled so much, and was so frightened, that he could no longer find voice or even breath to beg for mercy.

The poor boy could only beg with his eyes; but the green fisherman, without even looking at him, rolled him over five or six times in the flour, covering him so completely that he looked like a puppet made of plaster. Then he took him by the head and . . .

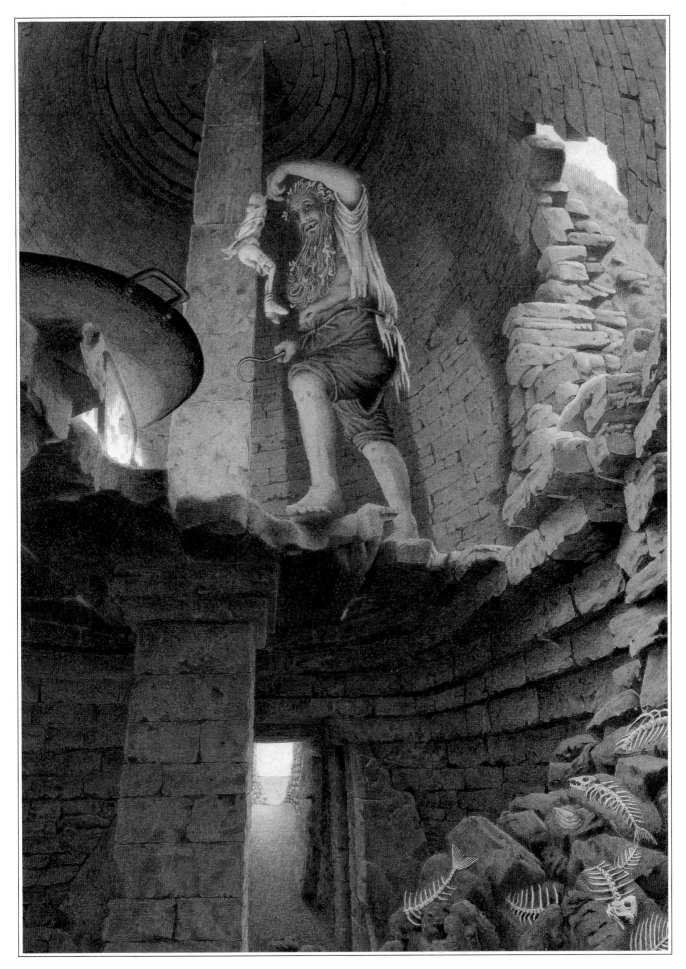

CHAPTER 29

Pinocchio goes back to the fairy's house;
she promises him that the next day
he will no longer be a puppet, but a boy;
grand breakfast of coffee and milk
to celebrate the coming event

Just as the fisherman was about to throw Pinocchio into the frying-pan, a big dog entered the cave, drawn there by the strong, delicious odour of fried fish.

"Get out!" ordered the fisherman, threatening him, and still holding the floury puppet in his hand.

But the poor dog was starving, and he howled, and wagged his tail as if to say, "Just give me one mouthful of fish, and I'll go away."

"Get out, I tell you!" repeated the fisherman, getting ready to kick him.

But the dog was far too hungry to care about being kicked, and growling at the fisherman, he showed his sharp teeth.

Just then, a faint little voice was heard in the cave saying, "Save me, Alidoro! If you don't save me, I shall be fried!"

The dog at once recognized Pinocchio's voice, and he was amazed to see that it came from that floury bundle in the fisherman's hand.

What did he do then? What do you think? He jumped, seized the bundle between his teeth and, holding it carefully, ran out of the cave and away like lightning.

The fisherman was terribly angry to see the fish he had so badly wanted to eat snatched from him, and he ran after the dog; but he had run only a few steps when he had a violent fit of coughing, and had to go back.

When Alidoro came to the road leading to the village, he stopped, and placed Pinocchio gently on the ground.

"How can I thank you?" said the puppet.

"No need to thank me," answered the dog. "You saved my life, and such a good turn deserves another. You know we must all help each other in this world."

"How did you come to the cave?"

"I was lying on the sand more dead than alive, when the wind brought me the odour of fried fish. An odour such as that gave me an appetite, and I followed it. If I had been later . . ."

"Don't speak of it!" yelled Pinocchio, who was still trembling with fear. "Don't mention it! If you had been later, I'd already have been fried, and eaten, and digested. B-r-r-r! It makes me shiver, just to think of it!"

Alidoro laughed, and held out his right paw to the puppet, who shook it heartily, as a sign of friendship, and then they parted.

The dog went home; but Pinocchio, when he was left alone, went to a little house near by, where an old man was sitting at the door, and said, "Tell me, good old man, do you know anything about a poor boy, Eugene, who was wounded on the head?"

"Some fishermen carried him to this house, but now . . ."

"Now he is dead!" interrupted Pinocchio, sadly.

"No, he is alive, and went home."

"Really? Truly?" cried the puppet, jumping for joy. "So, then, his wound wasn't serious?"

"It might have been very serious; it might have killed him," answered the old man, "for they threw a heavy book at his head." "Who threw it?"

"One of his schoolmates, a certain Pinocchio."

"Who is this Pinocchio?" inquired the puppet, as if he had never heard of him.

"They say he's a very bad boy, a vagabond, and a perfect good-for-nothing."

"Slander! Pure slander!"

"Do you know this Pinocchio?"

"I know him by sight," replied the puppet.

"And what do you think of him?" asked the old man.

"I think he is a very good boy, eager to study; he is obedient, and loves his father and his family."

While telling all these fibs, the puppet touched his nose and, seeing that it had grown several inches, he grew very frightened, and cried, "No, no, don't believe what I have said! I know Pinocchio very well, and can assure you he's a very bad boy. He is idle, and disobedient, and instead of going to school he amuses himself in the society of evil companions."

As soon as he had said this, his nose grew shorter, as short as it was to begin with.

"Why are you so white?" asked the old man suddenly.

"I'll tell you. Without noticing it, I rubbed myself against a wall that had just been whitewashed," answered the puppet, for he was ashamed to confess that he had been floured like a fish, prepared for being fried.

"But what happened to your jacket, and your trousers, and your cap?"

"I met with thieves, and they robbed me of my clothes. Do you happen to have some old clothes you could give me? Then I could go home."

"My child, I have nothing but a little bag in which I keep beans; if you want to have it, take it. You are welcome to it."

There was no need to ask Pinocchio twice. He took the little bag and, cutting one hole in the bottom, with the scissors, and one on each side for his arms, he put it on like a shirt. And, in that rough garb, he started for home.

But as he went he began to feel very uncomfortable. He took one step forward, and then one backward, saying to himself, "How can I ever approach that kind fairy? What will she say when she sees me? Will she forgive this second naughtiness? I don't think she will. Oh, I'm sure she won't. And it serves me right, for I am a wicked boy – always promising to better myself, and never keeping my word.''

It was night when he reached that village and very dark. As it was a stormy night, and was raining heavily, he went direct to the fairy's house, resolved to knock at the door, knowing he would be let in.

But when he came to the door he was frightened to knock, and ran back some distance. He came to the door a second time, but could not make a final decision; a third time – it was just the same. The fourth time he seized the iron knocker and, trembling, let it fall very lightly.

He waited, and waited, and at last, after waiting half an hour, a window was opened on the top floor (the house had four floors) and a big snail with a tiny light on her head looked out, and said, "Who is there, at this hour?"

"Is the fairy at home?" asked the puppet.

"The fairy is asleep and you mustn't disturb her. But who are you?"

"I am I."

"I? Who is I?"

"Pinocchio."

"Who is Pinocchio?"

"The puppet who lives with the fairy."

"Ah, I see!" said the snail. "Wait for me. I'll come down at once, and open the door."

"Hurry, for pity's sake! I am dying of cold."

"My lad, I am a snail, and snails are never in a hurry."

An hour passed; then two hours, but the door was not opened. Pinocchio, who was wet and shivering with cold and fright, gathered all his courage and knocked again, a little louder.

At this a window opened on the third floor, and the same snail looked out.

"Dear little snail," cried Pinocchio from the street, "I have been waiting two hours! And two hours in this awful weather seems longer than two years. Hurry up, for Heaven's sake!"

"My lad," said the sluggish, calm snail, "my lad, I am a snail, and snails are never in a hurry." And the window was closed.

Not long after, the clock struck midnight; then one o'clock, two o'clock; but the door was still closed.

At last Pinocchio lost his patience. In a rage, he seized the knocker to strike a blow that would shake the whole house; but suddenly the iron knocker turned into an eel and, slipping out of his hands, disappeared in the stream that was running in the street.

"Oh – ho!" shouted Pinocchio, blind with rage. "If the knocker can run away, I can kick the door." And drawing back, he gave a huge kick against the door. He kicked so hard that his foot went through the wood and, when he tried to pull it back, he couldn't. His foot was embedded in the door as firmly as a nail driven by a hammer.

Imagine poor Pinocchio! He had to spend the rest of the night with one foot

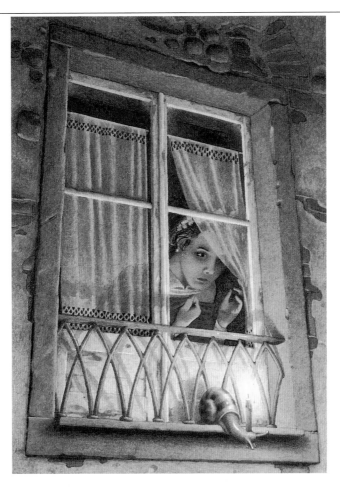

on the ground, and the other in the door.

Finally, at dawn the door was opened. That kind snail had spent only nine hours coming down from the fourth storey to the door. She must have been in a terrible hurry!

"What are you doing there, with your foot in the door?" she asked, laughing.

"It was an accident. Won't you try, kind snail, to free me from this trouble?"

"My lad, this is a job for a carpenter, and I have never been a carpenter."

"Beg the fairy to help me."

"The fairy is sleeping, and mustn't be disturbed."

"But what can I do all day, stuck to this door?"

"You can amuse yourself counting the ants that are passing by."

"At least bring me something to eat, for I am terribly hungry."

"At once!" said the snail.

In fact, three and a half hours later Pinocchio saw her coming back with a silver tray on her head, holding some bread, a roast chicken, and four ripe apricots.

"Here is the breakfast the fairy sends you," said the snail.

Seeing all those good things, the puppet was quite relieved. But how disappointed he grew when he discovered that the bread was plaster, the chicken made of board, and the four apricots coloured alabaster.

He wanted to cry, and, in his despair, he tried to throw away the tray and all that was on it; but instead, owing to his grief and his great weakness, he fainted.

When he came to himself, he was lying on a sofa, and the fairy was beside him.

"I shall forgive you once more," said the fairy, "but never more if you misbehave again."

Pinocchio vowed and promised that he would study, and always be good; and he kept his word for the rest of the year. He was first in the examinations, and became the best scholar in the school. His conduct was so satisfactory and praiseworthy that the fairy was very pleased, and said, "Tomorrow your wish shall be granted."

"Do you mean . . .?"

"Tomorrow you shall cease to be a wooden puppet, and become a real boy."

No one, without seeing Pinocchio at the moment he heard this longed-for news, can imagine his joy. All his classmates were invited to the fairy's house the next day, for a grand breakfast to celebrate the important event. The fairy prepared two hundred cups of coffee with cream, and four hundred bread rolls, buttered on both sides. The day promised to be a most happy and pleasant one, but . . .

Unfortunately, in the lives of puppets a *"but"* always spoils everything.

CHAPTER 30

Pinocchio listens to his friend Lampwick,
who is going to Playland

As one would expect, Pinocchio asked permission from the fairy to go to the village and invite his friends for the next day.

The fairy said, "Yes, by all means, go and invite your friends for breakfast, but remember to be back before dark. Do you understand?"

"I promise to be back in an hour," said the puppet.

"Be careful, Pinocchio. Children make promises very easily, but they are not so ready to keep their promises."

"But I'm different from other children; when I say a thing, I do it."

"We shall see. This time, if you are disobedient, so much the worse for you."

"Why?"

"Because children who do not follow the advice of those who are wiser than they are always come to grief."

"But I have learnt my lesson!" said Pinocchio. "And I shall never blunder again."

"We shall see if that's true."

The puppet said not a word more, kissed the good fairy, who was like a mother to him, and ran out of the house singing and dancing.

In less than an hour he had invited all his friends. Some of them accepted at once, with pleasure. Others waited to be urged; but when they heard that the rolls, which were to be dipped in the coffee and milk, would be buttered on both sides, they all said, "Yes, we'll come too, to please you."

Now you must know that Pinocchio had, among his schoolmates, one favourite of whom he was very fond. His name was Romeo, but everybody called him by his nickname, Lampwick, because he was so thin, and bright, just like a new wick on a night-lamp.

Lampwick was the laziest and most mischievous boy in the school, but Pinocchio liked him none the less. In fact, he went to him first of all, but he was not at home. He went back a second time, but no Lampwick; a third time, but still in vain.

Where could he be? He searched for him everywhere, and finally he found him hiding under the porch of a peasant's house.

"What are you doing there?" asked Pinocchio, creeping under the porch.

"I'm waiting for midnight, when I'm going . . ."

"Where are you going?"

"Far, very far away."

"I went to your place three times looking for you."

"What do you want with me?"

"Have you not heard the great news? Don't you know of my good fortune?"

"What?"

"From tomorrow I shall no longer be a puppet but a boy like you, and the other boys."

"Much good may it do you!"

"And tomorrow I expect you at my house for breakfast."

"But didn't I tell you that I'm going away tonight?"

"At what time?"

"At midnight."

"Where are you going?"

"I'm going to live in a country – the most beautiful country in the world – a real dreamland."

"What's its name?"

"It's called Playland. Why don't you come too?"

"I? Certainly not!"

"You are wrong, Pinocchio! Believe me, if you don't come, you will be sorry. Where could you find a better place for us boys? There's no school there, no masters, and no books. In that heavenly place, no one ever studies. There's no school on Saturday; and in every week there are six Saturdays, and one Sunday. Just imagine! The autumn holidays begin in January, and last until the thirty-first of December. Now, a place like that is the ideal place to live in! That's how all civilized countries should be run."

"But how do they pass the time in Playland?"

"How? Play and amuse themselves from morning till night. Then they go to bed, and start again next morning. What do you think of that?"

"Um!" said Pinocchio, and shook his head as if to say, "That sort of life wouldn't be too bad!"

"Now then, will you come, or won't you? Yes, or no? Make up your mind!"

"No, no, no, and finally no! I promised the good fairy to be a good boy, and I must keep my promise. In fact, it's nearly evening, so I must leave you and hurry back. Good-bye, and a pleasant journey!"

"Where are you going in such a hurry?"

"I'm going home. The good fairy wants me to be home before dark."

"Wait a little longer."

"I shall be too late."

"Just two minutes."

"And if the fairy scolds me?"

"Let her scold. When she's done scolding, she'll stop," said that rascal of a Lampwick.

"How are you going? Alone, or in company?"

"Alone? There'll be more than a hundred boys with me!"

"Are you going on foot?"

"A stagecoach is coming soon to take us to that dream country."

"What wouldn't I give if the coach were coming right now!"

"Why?"

"Because I could see you all starting together."

"Stay a little longer, and you can do so."

"No, no, I must go."

"Wait just two more minutes."

"I've waited too long already. The fairy won't know what's happened to me."

"Poor fairy! Is she afraid the bats will eat you?"

"No, no. But . . ." continued Pinocchio, "are you absolutely sure there are no schools in that country?"

"Not a single one!"

"And no masters?"

"Not one."

"And no one ever has to study?"

"Never, never, never!"

"What a beautiful country!" sighed Pinocchio. "Of course I've never been there, but I can imagine what it must be like."

"Why don't you come, then?"

"It's useless to tempt me. I've promised the good fairy to be an obedient boy, and I shall not break my word."

"Well, good-bye then, and give my love to the boys at the schools – and to all the high schools, too, if you meet them on the street."

"Good-bye, Lampwick. I wish you a pleasant journey. I hope you'll have a fine time, and think of your friends now and then."

Saying this the puppet took a few steps but then stopped and, turning to his friend, he asked, "Are you quite sure that there are six Saturdays and one Sunday in a week?"

"Quite."

"Are you sure, but really sure that holidays begin on the first of January, and end on the thirty-first of December?"

"Perfectly sure."

"What a wonderful country!" said Pinocchio again, delightedly. Then he added quickly with a final resolution, "Well, good-bye, and I hope you have a good journey!"

"Good-bye."

"How long before you start?"

"A little over an hour."

"A pity! If it were only one hour, I could perhaps be tempted to wait and see you off."

"And the fairy?"

"I've waited so long already, an hour more or less wouldn't matter."

"Poor Pinocchio! And if the fairy scolds you?"

"Never mind! I'd let her scold. When she's done scolding she'll stop."

Meanwhile, it grew very dark. Suddenly they saw a little light moving, in the distance, and heard bells tinkling, people talking and the hooting of a horn, very faint and low, like the humming of a wasp.

"There it is!" exclaimed Lampwick, jumping to his feet.

"What is it?" Pinocchio asked softly.

"It's the coach coming for me. Do you want to come too? Yes, or no?"

"But is it true," asked the puppet, "that children never have to study in that country?"

"Never, never, never!"

"What a wonderful country! What a beautiful country! What a marvellous country!"

CHAPTER 31

*Pinocchio goes away to Playland,
where he spends five months*

At last the coach arrived, without making the least noise, for the wheels were padded with rags and tow.

It was drawn by twelve pairs of donkeys, all the same size, but of different colours. Some were grey, some white, some spotted, others again were yellow and blue in large stripes.

But the funniest thing about them was that these twelve pairs, that is twenty-four donkeys, were not shod like other animals; they had on men's boots of white leather.

And the driver?

Imagine a small man broader than he is long, soft and greasy as butter, with a small face like a red tomato, a little mouth that is always laughing, and a soft, caressing voice, like that of a cat that is mewing to the lady of the house for cream.

All the boys took a great fancy to him as soon as they saw him; and they all hurried to get in first, and go to that most delightful country known on the map as True Playland.

The coach was already full of boys between eight and twelve years old, pressed together like salted fish in a barrel. They were crowded and uncomfortable, and they could hardly breathe, but no one said a word. No one complained. The consolation of knowing that in a few hours they would be in a land where there were no books, or schools, or masters, made them accept anything; and they were so happy that they did not feel discomfort, weariness, hunger, thirst, or sleepiness.

As soon as the coach stopped, the little man turned to Lampwick and, with many bows and grimaces, said to him, smiling, "Tell me, my fine lad, would you also like to go to that happy country?"

"I want to go, most certainly."

"But as you see, my dear lad, there is no room; the coach is full."

"It doesn't matter," replied Lampwick. "If there's no room inside, I'll find some place on the crossbar." And he jumped up astride the crossbar.

"And you, my love," said the little man, addressing Pinocchio, with a flattering smile, "what are you going to do? Are you coming or staying behind?"

"I'm staying here," answered Pinocchio, "for I am going home. I want to study and be a very good scholar, like all well-brought-up boys."

"Much good may it do you!"

"Pinocchio," cried Lampwick, "listen to me! Come with us! We'll have a marvellous time."

"No, no, no!"

"Come with us! We'll have lots of fun!" shouted some voices inside the coach.

"Come with us! We'll all be happy!" shouted hundreds of voices together.

"If I come with you, what would my good fairy say?" continued Pinocchio.

"Don't worry about that. Think only that we are going to a country where we'll have nothing but fun from morning till night."

Pinocchio did not answer; he only sighed. He sighed a second time, a third time, and at last he said, "Make a little room for me. I am coming."

"Everything is full," replied the little man, "but to show you how happy I am that you're with us, I shall give you my place."

"And what will you do?"

"I shall walk."

"No, I can't let you do that. I'd rather ride on one of the donkeys!" cried Pinocchio.

So saying, he went up to the donkey harnessed to the right-hand side of the shaft, and wanted to jump on his back, but the beast turned and kicked him in the stomach, sending him sprawling with his legs in the air.

Think of all those impertinent boys, nearly bursting with laughter.

But the little man did not laugh. He went to that kicking donkey and, pretending to give him a kiss, he bit off half his right ear.

While he was doing this Pinocchio, still angry, got up from the ground and, with one leap, jumped on the donkey's back. He jumped so splendidly that all the boys stopped laughing, and shouted, "Hurrah, Pinocchio!" and applauded as if they would never stop.

But suddenly the donkey kicked so high with his hind legs that he threw the poor puppet on to a heap of stones.

The boys laughed at him again; but the little man, instead of laughing, went to the other side of the kicking beast, and bit off half of his left ear.

Then he told the puppet, "Now get on his back. You needn't be frightened. That donkey is very obstinate; but I've whispered something in his ear, and I think he'll be obedient and gentle now."

Pinocchio mounted again, and the coach started to move; but while the donkeys galloped and the coach rolled over the paving stones, he thought he heard a voice which was so low that he could hardly hear the words, saying, "You poor fool! You decided to do as you please, but you'll be sorry for it!"

Pinocchio was frightened, and looked around to see where these words came from, but he could see nothing. The donkeys galloped, the stage-coach rolled over the stones, and the boys inside slept. Lampwick snored like a bear; and the little man sang between his teeth,

III

Everybody sleeps through the night
While I never sleep . . .

A little way farther on Pinocchio heard again the low voice saying, "Remember this, you fool – boys who won't study, and who desert their school, their books, and their masters, always come to a bad end. I have tried it, and I know what I am talking about. The day will come when you will weep as I am weeping now; but then it will be too late!"

When he heard these whispered words, the puppet was more frightened than ever. He jumped down from the donkey's back, and took him by the bridle.

Imagine his surprise when he saw that the donkey was crying, just like a boy.

"Hullo, little man," Pinocchio called the driver. "Did you ever see such a thing? This donkey is crying."

"Let him cry! He can laugh on Tib's Eve."

"Did you teach him to talk?"

"No, he taught himself to mumble a few words when he was in a company of trained dogs for three years."

"Poor beast!"

"Come, come!" said the little man. "Don't waste time watching a donkey cry. Get on to him again, and let us go! The night is cold and the way is long."

Pinocchio obeyed without another word. The coach rolled along again, and at dawn they arrived safely at Playland.

Playland was like no other country in the world. The population consisted of children. The eldest was fourteen, and the youngest scarcely eight years old. The merriment and shouting and noise in the streets were maddening.

There were children everywhere. Some were playing skittles, some quoits, cycling or ball, some were riding on wooden horses; others were playing blind-man's buff, or chasings; some were dressed as clowns, and were eating burning tow; some were acting, or singing, or reading, or turning somersaults; others were walking on their hands, while still others were trundling hoops or, dressed like generals, were marching along with paper helmets ordering troops of soldiers about. There was laughing, and shouting, and hand-clapping; some were whistling; some were clucking like a hen that has just laid an egg. In short, there was such noise and confusion that, without cotton wool in both ears, anyone would have been deafened by it. There were theatres, crowded all day long, in every open space, and on all the walls of the houses, badly spelt remarks had been scribbled with charcoal.

Immediately they got inside the city, Lampwick, and the other boys who had come together, hurried to join the children, and very soon, as you may well imagine, they became excellent friends. Who could be happier, or more contented, than they?

Amidst continual games and all sorts of pastimes, hours, days and weeks passed like lightning.

"Oh, what a beautiful life!" shouted Pinocchio, every time he met Lampwick.

"Do you at last see that I was right?" answered Lampwick. "And to think you didn't want to come! To think you intended going back to your fairy, and wasting your time in studying! If you are free today from nasty books and schools, you owe it to me, to my advice, to my insistence. It's only a real friend who would show such kindness."

"Yes, that's true, Lampwick! If today I am a really happy boy, I owe it all to you. And do you know what the master used to say to me about you? He always said, 'Don't have anything to do with that good-for-nothing Lampwick. He is a very bad boy, and will lead you into some trouble'."

"Poor old master!" said the other, shaking his head. "I well know that he didn't like me, and spoke ill of me. But I have a generous soul, and with pleasure I forgive him."

"Noble boy!" said Pinocchio, embracing his friend, and kissing him affectionately on the forehead.

Five months had passed in this playland, of toys and amusements which went on all day long, without ever seeing a book or even the outside of a school, when Pinocchio, upon awakening one morning, had a very unpleasant surprise, and lost his good spirits.

CHAPTER 32

*Pinocchio gets donkey's ears,
and then becomes a real donkey
and starts to bray*

And what was this surprise?

I shall tell you, my dear readers. The surprise was that Pinocchio, when he woke up, scratched his head; and while doing so he noticed . . .

Can you make any guess as to what he noticed?

He noticed, to his great amazement, that his ears had grown several inches.

You must know that puppets from their birth have very small ears; in fact so small that they are invisible to the naked eye. So you can imagine how surprised he was when he noticed that his ears had grown so long during the night that they looked like two brooms. He hurried to find a mirror, that he might see himself; but he could not find one. So he filled his wash basin with water, looked into it, and saw what he had been hoping never to see. He saw himself decorated with a magnificent pair of donkey's ears.

Can you imagine poor Pinocchio's sorrow, shame, and despair?

He began to cry, and scream, and beat his head against the wall; but the more he cried, the longer his ears grew, and they became hairy at the top.

A charming little squirrel that lived on the floor above him, hearing his loud cries, came down to see what the matter was; and, seeing the puppet in such a state, she asked earnestly, "What's happened to you, my dear neighbour?"

"I am sick, dear squirrel, I am very sick – and of such an awful disease. Do you know how to count a pulse?"

"Yes, I think so."

"Then will you please see if I have a fever?"

The squirrel put her right forepaw on Pinocchio's pulse, and then said with a sigh, "My friend, I am very sorry, but I have bad news for you."

"What is it?"

"You have a very dangerous fever."

"What kind of fever is it?"

"Donkey fever."

"I never heard of such a fever!" said the puppet, though he knew well what she meant.

"Then I shall explain it to you," answered the squirrel, "for you must know that in a few hours you will no longer be a puppet, or a boy . . ."

"What will I be?"

"In a few hours you will be a real donkey, like those that draw carts, or carry cabbages and vegetables to the market."

"Oh, poor me! Poor me!" cried Pinocchio, seizing his ears with his hands, and pulling and jerking them, as if they belonged to somebody else.

"My dear lad," said the squirrel, wishing to console him, "you can't do anything. It is your destiny. For it is written in the decrees above that lazy children who dislike books, schools, and masters, and who spend their time with toys, games, and amusements, must end up, sooner or later, by becoming little donkeys."

"Is that really true?" sobbed Pinocchio.

"It is, unhappily. It's no use crying now. You should have thought of that before it was too late."

"But it's not my fault. Believe me, little squirrel, it's all Lampwick's fault!"

"Who is Lampwick?"

"One of my schoolmates. I wanted to go home; I wanted to be good; I wanted to study and never do any mischief; but Lampwick said, 'Why should you bother about studying? Why do you want to go to school? Instead, come with me to Playland. There we shall never study; we shall only play from morning till evening, and always be happy!'"

"Why did you listen to that false friend – to that bad companion?"

"Because . . . because, dear little squirrel, I am a heartless puppet, with no sense. Oh, if I had had just a little bit of heart, I'd never have abandoned that kind fairy who loved me as a mother, and who had done so much for me! And now I could be a real boy, like the others, instead of a puppet! Oh, if I meet Lampwick, he'll get it! I'll fix him!"

He wanted to leave the room, but at the door he remembered his ears, and he was ashamed to show them. So then what do you think he did? He took a large cotton cap, and pulled it over his head, right down to his nose.

Then he went out, and looked for Lampwick. He searched the streets, the squares, and theatres, everywhere, but he could not find him. He turned to everyone he met, but no one had seen him. At last he went to his house and knocked at the door.

"Who's there?" asked Lampwick, from inside.

"Pinocchio," said the puppet.

"Just a minute, and I'll let you in."

After half an hour the door was opened. Imagine Pinocchio's surprise, when he went in and found that his friend Lampwick had a great cotton cap on his head which came down over the end of his nose.

Seeing that, Pinocchio felt somewhat better, and he said to himself, "Perhaps he has the same sickness as I have. Can it be possible that he, too, has the donkey fever?"

He pretended not to see anything, and said, smiling, "How are you, my dear Lampwick?"

"Very well. As well as a mouse in a Parmesan cheese."

"Do you really mean it?"

"I have no reason to tell you a lie."

"Excuse me, my friend, but why then do you wear a cap that covers your ears?"

"The doctor ordered it, because I've hurt my knee. And you, dear puppet, why do you wear a cotton cap down over your nose?"

"The doctor prescribed it, because I hurt my leg."

"Oh, poor Pinocchio!"

"Oh, poor Lampwick!"

They kept silent for a long while and the two friends looked knowingly at each other.

At last the puppet said, in a sweet voice full of persuasion, "Just to satisfy my curiosity, dear Lampwick, have you ever had any trouble with your ears?"

"Never! And you?"

"Never! Except that one of my ears was aching this morning."

"Yes, so was mine."

"Yours, too? Which one aches?"

"Both of them. And yours?"

"Both of them. Do you think we have the same sickness?"

"I'm afraid I do."

"Will you do me a favour, Lampwick?"

"Yes, with the greatest pleasure."

"Will you let me see your ears?"

"Why not? But first I'd like to see yours, dear Pinocchio."

"No, you be the first."

"No, dear fellow. You first, and then I'll show mine."

"Well," said the puppet, "let us agree, like good friends."

"What to?"

"We'll take off our caps at the same time. Agreed?"

"Agreed."

"Then, ready!" And Pinocchio began to count in a loud voice, "One! Two! Three!"

At "Three!" they took off their caps, and threw them in the air.

And then something happened that sounds unbelievable, yet it was true. When Pinocchio and Lampwick saw that the same misfortune had befallen them both, instead of being ashamed and despairing, they tried to wag their long ears, and finished by laughing at each other.

They laughed and laughed, until they nearly exploded.

But suddenly Lampwick stopped laughing. He staggered and grew pale as he spoke to his friend, "Help, help, Pinocchio!"

"What's the trouble?"

"Alas! I can't stand up straight."

"Neither can I," cried Pinocchio, tottering and weeping.

While talking, they bent down on all fours, and started running round the room on their hands and feet. As they ran, their hands became hoofs, their faces grew as long as muzzles, and their backs were covered by light grey hair with black spots.

But the most dreadful and the most humiliating moment for those two miserable boys was when they felt their tails growing. Overcome by shame and sorrow, they began to cry, and lament over their fate.

Oh, if they had only kept quiet! Instead of sighs and lamentations, they brayed like donkeys. Yes, both together, in chorus, they brayed loudly.

Meanwhile somebody knocked at the door, and a voice shouted, "Open the door! I am the little man, the driver who brought you here. Open at once, or it will be the worse for you!"

CHAPTER 33

As Pinocchio becomes a real donkey,
he is sold to the manager of a show and learns
how to dance and jump through a hoop;
but he is lamed one evening,
and then is bought by a man who decides to
make a drum of his skin

As they did not open the door, the little man kicked it open, and addressed Pinocchio and Lampwick with his usual laugh.

"Hurrah for you! You brayed very well; I recognized your voices at once. And now, here I am."

At these words the two donkeys became silent, their heads were hanging down, and their tails between their legs.

At first the little man stroked and patted them; then drawing forth a curry-comb, he combed them well. When they were shiny so that he could see his face in them, he bridled them, and took them to market, hoping to sell them at a profit.

Indeed, buyers were not lacking. Lampwick was sold to a farmer whose donkey had died the day before; and Pinocchio was bought by the manager of a company of clowns and rope-walkers, who intended teaching him to jump and dance, together with the other animals belonging to the company.

Now you can see, my little readers, what a fine business the little man carried on? He was a cruel little monster, seemingly all milk and honey, going round the world with his coach. By promises and flattery he collected all the children who did not like their books, and did not want to go to school. When his coach was full he carried the children off to Playland, so that they might spend their time amusing themselves. When these poor children, from endless playing and lack of studying, became so many donkeys, he took them to market and sold them happily. In a few years, by this means, he earned a lot of money, and became a millionaire.

I do not know what happened to Lampwick, but I know that Pinocchio, from the very first moment, led a hard life full of drudgery.

When he was led into the stable, his master put straw in his manger, but Pinocchio spat it out after he had tasted it.

Then his master, grumbling, put some hay in the manger; but Pinocchio did not like that either.

"Ah! You don't even like hay?" shouted his master, full of anger. "Leave it to me, my fine donkey! If you are so fussy, I know how to cure you!" And he beat his legs with his whip for a start.

The pain made Pinocchio cry, and bray, "Ee-a! I can't digest straw!"

"Then eat hay," replied his master, who understood donkey dialect perfectly.

"Ee-a! Hay gives me the stomach ache!"

"Do you want to tell me I have to feed a donkey like you on chicken breasts and capon jelly?" said his master, growing still more angry, whipping him again and again.

After this second whipping Pinocchio thought it would be wiser to keep silent, and he said no more. The stable door was shut, and Pinocchio remained alone. As it was so long since he had eaten anything, hunger made him yawn; and when he yawned he opened his mouth as large as an oven. At last, as there was nothing but hay in his manger, he decided to eat it, and after chewing it a long time, he shut his eyes and swallowed it.

"This hay isn't so bad," he said. "But how much better it would have been if I'd gone on with my studies! Instead of hay, I might now be eating the crusty end of a fresh loaf of bread, with a fine slice of sausage! No matter!"

In the morning, he looked again for a little hay; but he found none, for he had eaten it all during the night.

Then he tried a mouthful of chopped straw, but as he chewed it he thought what a difference there was between the taste of chopped straw, and rice, or macaroni.

"No matter!" he said again, as he went on chewing. "I hope my misfortune will serve as a lesson to disobedient children who don't like studying. No matter! No matter!"

"Why 'No matter'?" shouted his master, who came into the stable at that moment. "Do you think, my dear donkey, that I bought you just to feed you? I bought you to do some work, and to help me make money. Get up, now, and do your best! Come into the circus, and I'll teach you to jump through a hoop, breaking the paper with your head; to dance, waltz and polka, and to stand on your hind legs."

So poor Pinocchio, by hook or by crook, had to learn all these fine tricks; but it took him three months, and he got many sharp cuts from the whip.

At last the day arrived when his master announced a really wonderful performance. Gaily coloured posters were placed at all the street corners, reading thus:

GRAND FULL-DRESS PERFORMANCE
TONIGHT
THE USUAL DARING FEATS

and

ASTONISHING PERFORMANCES

by

ALL THE ARTISTS

and by all the HORSES of the Company

IN ADDITION

The First Appearance of the Famous

LITTLE DONKEY

PINOCCHIO

called

THE STAR of the DANCE

The Theatre will be brilliantly illuminated

You may believe me the theatre was full an hour before the opening of the show.

Not one more seat could have been bought, even for its weight in gold. The seats round the ring were packed with girls and boys, impatient to see the famous little donkey Pinocchio dancing.

After the first part of the show, the ringmaster came forward. He was wearing a black coat, with white tights, and boots reaching above his knees. After a deep bow, he made the following ridiculous speech:

"Honoured public, ladies and gentlemen!

"The humble undersigned, staying temporarily in your city, wishes to have the honour, not less than the pleasure, of presenting to this intelligent and distinguished audience a famous little donkey, who has had the honour of dancing before the sovereigns of all the principal courts of Europe.

"I thank you for listening attentively to me, and beg that you assist us with your inspiring presence, and find excuses for our shortcomings."

This speech was received with much laughter and applause; but the applause redoubled, and became tempestuous, when the Little Donkey Pinocchio appeared in the middle of the ring. He was magnificently decked out! He had a new bridle of shiny leather, with brass buckles and studs, and white camellias behind his ears. His mane was divided into small curls, each one decorated with coloured silk ribbons, a broad band of gold and silver surrounded his body, and his tail was braided with crimson and blue velvet ribbons. In fact, he was a lovely little donkey.

Presenting him to the public the manager added these words: "Honourable

audience! I am not here to tell you untrue stories about the great difficulties I had to conquer in order to capture and subjugate this mammal, as he was feeding, wild and free, in the mountains and plains of the torrid zone. Observe, I beseech you, the ferocious gleams in his eyes. After every tender means of taming him failed, I was forced to use the last resort, the whip. Yet all my kindness, which should have increased his love for me, only made him fiercer day by day. However, following the system of Gall, I found on his cranium a bump, which the Faculty of Medicine in Paris declared to be the generator of hair and of dance. Therefore, I have taught him to dance, and also to jump through hoops and frames covered with paper. Admire him, and judge him! But before I take my leave of you, permit me, ladies and gents, to invite you to the performance of tomorrow evening. Should bad weather threaten, then the show, instead of tomorrow evening, will be set back to tomorrow, at eleven o'clock in the a.m.''

Here the ringmaster bowed once again and then, turning to Pinocchio, he said, "Come, Pinocchio! Before you start your performance, salute this distinguished audience – ladies, gentlemen, and children!"

Pinocchio obediently bent his knees, and remained kneeling until the ringmaster cracked his whip, and shouted, "Walk!"

Then the little donkey got up and walked round the ring.

After a while the ringmaster shouted, "Trot!" Pinocchio obeyed the order, and started to trot.

"Gallop!"

And Pinocchio broke into a gallop.

"Run!"

And Pinocchio ran as fast as he could.

Suddenly, while he raced round the ring, the ringmaster raised his arm in the air and fired off a pistol.

At that the donkey, pretending to be wounded, fell down as if he were dead.

As he rose up, amid applause and clapping of hands, he lifted his head and looked up at the people; and there he saw, in one of the boxes, a beautiful lady who wore a heavy gold chain round her neck, from which hung a medallion. On the medallion was the portrait of a puppet.

"That is my portrait! The lady is the fairy!" said Pinocchio to himself, recognizing her immediately.

He was so overcome with joy that he tried to cry, "Oh, my dear fairy! Oh, my dear fairy!" But instead of these words, there came forth from his throat a bray – so long and loud that everyone present laughed, and especially the children.

Then the ringmaster, to teach him that it was not good manners to bray like that before the public, struck him on the nose with the handle of his whip.

The poor little donkey put out his tongue, and licked his nose at least five minutes to ease the pain he felt.

But how great was his disappointment when, turning to the box again, he saw that it was empty. The fairy had disappeared!

He thought he was going to die; his eyes were full of tears and he began to cry bitterly.

However, no one noticed it; least of all the ringmaster, who, cracking his whip, shouted, "Courage, Pinocchio! Now show this gracious audience how elegantly you can leap through the hoop."

Pinocchio tried two or three times; but each time he came to the hoop, he thought it easier to run under, than through it. At last he leaped through it; but his right hind-leg caught in the hoop, and he fell heavily to the ground on the other side.

When he got up he was lame, and could walk back to the stable only with great difficulty.

"Bring out Pinocchio! We want the little donkey! Bring out the little donkey!" shouted the children, who were all very sorry about his accident.

But the little donkey did not appear any more that evening.

When the veterinary surgeon – that is, the animal doctor – saw him the next morning, he declared that he would stay lame for the rest of his life.

Then the ringmaster said to his stable boy, "What can I do with a lame donkey? Why should I feed him if he can't work? Take him to the market and sell him."

As soon as they came to the market they found a buyer who asked the boy, "How much do you want for this lame donkey?"

"Five crowns."

"I'll give you fivepence. You mustn't think I'm buying him for use. I'm buying him only for his skin. I see he has a very hard skin, and I want to make a drum for the village band."

You can imagine how Pinocchio must have felt when he heard that he was to be a drum!

As soon as the fivepence was paid, the new owner led the little donkey to a rock by the shore, tied a stone to his neck, and a long rope to one leg. Then he gave him a sudden push, and Pinocchio fell into the water.

Pinocchio, with that stone on his neck, went immediately to the bottom; and his owner, holding the rope tight, sat down on the rock to wait until the donkey was drowned, so that he might skin him.

CHAPTER 34

Pinocchio, thrown into the sea and eaten by the fish,
becomes a puppet again;
but, while swimming towards dry land,
he is swallowed by a terrible shark

When the little donkey had been underwater about an hour, his new owner said to himself, "That poor little lame donkey must surely be drowned by this time! I'll pull him up, and make a fine drum of his skin."

He began hauling in the rope he had tied to the donkey's leg. He hauled, and hauled, and hauled, and at last there appeared on the water . . . what do you think? Instead of a dead donkey, there was a live puppet, wriggling like an eel.

When he saw that wooden puppet, the poor man thought he was dreaming. He was struck dumb and, astonished, he stood there with his mouth open, and his eyes starting out of his head.

When he recovered a little, he could only stammer, "Where . . . where is the little donkey I threw into the water? What happened to him?"

"I am the little donkey!" answered the puppet, laughing.

"You!"

"I!"

"Ah, you scallywag, don't play any tricks on me!"

"Play tricks on you? Nothing of the sort, my dear master; I am very serious."

"But how can it be that you, who were a little donkey a short while ago, have now become a wooden puppet?"

"It must be due to the sea water. It does, sometimes, work real miracles."

"Be careful, puppet! Don't try to pull my leg! You'll get it if I lose my patience!"

"Well, master, do you want to hear my true story? If you free my leg from this rope, I'll tell it to you."

The good man was very curious to hear his true story, so he quickly freed his leg, and Pinocchio, free as a bird once more, began to speak as follows:

"You must know that I was once a wooden puppet, just as I am now; and I was on the verge of becoming a real boy, like so many others. The trouble started because I didn't like to study, and I listened to evil companions, and so I ran away from home. One day I woke up to find myself a donkey, with long ears and a long tail. Oh, I was so ashamed of myself! Oh, dear master, I hope the good Saint Antony will keep you from ever being ashamed! I was taken to the market with the other donkeys, and sold to the ringmaster of a circus. He taught me to dance and leap through a hoop; but one evening, during the performance, I fell, and my leg got lamed. The ringmaster had no use for a lame donkey, so he sent me to the market, and you bought me.''

''I well know that, since I paid fivepence for you. And now, who will give me back my poor pennies?''

''And why did you buy me! To make a drum out of my skin! A drum!''

''That's true! And now where shall I find another skin?''

''Don't despair, master! There are so many little donkeys in this world.''

''Well, you impertinent urchin, is that the end of your story?''

''No,'' answered the puppet. ''A couple more words, and I'll have finished. After buying me, you brought me here to kill me; and as you pitied me, you preferred to tie a stone to my neck, and throw me into the sea. This humane sentiment counts to your credit, and I shall be grateful to you for ever, my dear master. You reckoned without the fairy.''

''And who is this fairy?''

''She is my mother and, like every mother, she loves her child dearly, and never loses sight of him, and helps him in all his troubles, even when, because of his foolishness and his naughty ways, he deserves no help. So, as I wanted to say, as soon as the good fairy saw I was in danger of drowning she sent an immense shoal of fish who thought that I was a dead donkey, and began to eat me. And what huge bites they took! I would never have believed that fish were greedier than boys! Some ate my ears, others my muzzle, others my neck and mane, my hoofs, and even the skin off my leg and off my back; and one of them was so polite that he condescended to eat my tail.''

''From this day forward,'' said this horrified buyer, ''I vow never to eat fish. It would be a pretty sight to open a mullet, or a whiting, and find a donkey's tail inside!''

''I agree with you,'' said the puppet, laughing; ''as for that, you must know that when the donkey's hide that covered me from head to foot, was eaten away, naturally the bones remained – or, to be exact, the wood; for, as you see, I am made of very hard wood. But after the first bite, the fish saw that there was no more meat to eat and, disgusted by such indigestible food, they swam off in all directions, without even saying thank you. That is why, when you hauled in the rope, you found a live puppet and not a dead donkey.''

''Enough of your story!'' shouted the man in a rage. ''I have paid fivepence for you, and I want my money back! Do you know what I'll do? I'll take you back to the market, and sell you for firewood.''

''Sell me if you want to. I don't mind,'' said Pinocchio.

But as he spoke, he made a big leap, and plunged into the sea; and as he swam gaily away he shouted to the poor buyer, ''Good-bye, master! When you want a skin to make a drum, remember me.'' He kept on laughing as he swam farther away.

After a little while he turned again, and shouted still louder, ''Good-bye, master! When you want a little nice dry firewood, remember me.''

In the twinkling of an eye he was so far away that he was hardly visible; in fact, there was only a black dot on the water when he now and then lifted an arm, or a leg, or jumped about like a joyful dolphin.

Pinocchio was swimming, not caring where he was going, when he saw in the sea a rock which looked like white marble. On the top of the rock a beautiful little goat was bleating, and beckoning to him to come nearer.

However, the strangest thing was, that the goat's fleece, instead of being white, or black, or a mixture of these two colours, as you find with other goats, was blue – a very bright blue, that reminded him of the hair of that lovely child.

Pinocchio's heart began to beat very quickly. Doubling his energy, he swam towards the white rock. He was already half-way there, when he saw, rushing towards him in the water, a sea monster with a horrible head, and its mouth, which was like a deep cave, wide open, with three rows of teeth that would have frightened anyone, even in a picture.

Do you know what this monster was?

It was no less than that gigantic shark, which has been mentioned more than once in this history, and which, owing to its dreadful killings and its ravenous greed, was called the "Attila of fish and fishermen".

Poor Pinocchio was terribly frightened seeing such a monster. He tried to dodge him, to swim elsewhere, or to swim faster than this monster; but that huge, gaping mouth came right after him, quickly as an arrow.

"Hurry, Pinocchio, for mercy's sake!" bleated the beautiful little goat.

Pinocchio swam desperately, using every ounce of his strength.

"Quickly, Pinocchio! The monster is close behind you!"

And Pinocchio swam faster than ever, swift as a ball from a gun. He was near the rock, and the little goat was leaning out over the sea, and stretching out her front legs to help him out of the water . . .

But it was too late! The monster had caught him and, drawing in his breath, he sucked him in as one sucks an egg. He sucked him in so fiercely and greedily, and Pinocchio fell so hard against the monster's stomach, that he lost consciousness for a quarter of an hour.

When he came to himself, he had no idea where he was. All around him it was very dark: the darkness was so thick and deep that he felt as if he had dived head first into a bottle full of ink. He listened, but he heard nothing: only from time to time, a great gust of wind blew in his face. At first he did not know where the wind came from, but he soon noticed that it came from the monster's lungs.

At first Pinocchio tried to be brave; but when he knew for certain that he was inside the shark's body, as in a prison, he began to weep and sob, "Help! Help! Oh poor me! Will no one come and save me?"

"Who could come to save you, you miserable wretch?" said a voice in the darkness, like a guitar out of tune.

"Who speaks?" asked Pinocchio, frozen with fear.

"It's I. I'm a poor tunny fish, who was swallowed at the same time as you. What sort of a fish are you?"

"I have nothing to do with fish. I'm a puppet."

"If you're not a fish, why did you come here that the monster should swallow you?"

"I didn't *come* here; he swallowed me. What are we going to do now, in this cellar?"

"We must resign ourselves, and wait for the shark to digest us."

"But I don't want to be digested!" shouted Pinocchio, beginning to cry again.

"Neither do I want to be digested!" said the tunny. "But I'm wise enough to console myself with the thought that when one is born a tunny, it's more dignified to die in the water than in oil."

"Stuff and nonsense!" cried Pinocchio.

"That is my opinion," replied the tunny. "And opinions, as our tunny politicians say, must be respected."

"However that may be, I want to get away from here. I want to escape . . ."

"Escape then, if you can!"

"This shark that has swallowed us, is he very big?"

"His body is more than a mile long, and I'm not counting his tail."

While they were talking in the darkness, Pinocchio thought he saw a gleam of light, very far away.

"What can that light be, that I see so far away?" asked Pinocchio.

"It's one of our fellows in misfortune, who, like us, is waiting to be digested."

"I'm going to find him. It might possibly be an old fish who could tell me how to get out of here."

"I hope so, dear puppet."

"Good-bye, tunny."

"Good-bye, puppet. Good luck to you."

"Where shall we meet again?"

"Who knows? Better not to think of it."

CHAPTER 35

Pinocchio finds in the body of the shark . . .
whom does he find?
Read this chapter, and you will know

Pinocchio, having said good-bye to the tunny, started feeling his way in the darkness through the shark's body, finding his way along, step by step, towards that dim, flickering light in the distance.

The farther he went the better he could see the little light. He walked and walked, and at last, when he reached it, what did he find? I shall give you a thousand guesses. He found a little table well prepared, with a lighted candle stuck in a green glass bottle; and sitting at the table there was a snow-white old man. He was eating some fish, which were so much alive that sometimes they jumped out of his mouth while he ate them.

Seeing the old man, poor Pinocchio suddenly felt so happy that he nearly fainted. He wanted to laugh, to cry, to say thousands of things; and instead he could only stammer some broken, senseless words.

At last he managed to utter a cry of joy and, opening his arms, he threw them around the old man's neck, shouting, "Oh, daddy! My daddy! Have I found you at last? I'll never leave you again – never, never, never!"

"So my eyes do not deceive me?" said the old man, rubbing them with both hands. "You are really my dear Pinocchio?"

"Yes, yes, it's really, truly me! Do you still remember me? O, my dear daddy, how good you are! And to think that I . . . Oh! but when you know how many things I've been through, and how many things have gone wrong . . . You know, dear daddy, that the very same day you sold your coat to buy me a primer so that I could go to school, I ran away to see the puppet show; and the Showman was ready to put me in the fire, the better to roast his mutton. It was the same man who gave me five gold pieces to bring to you, but I met the fox and the cat, and they took me to the Lobster Inn, where they gobbled up everything like hungry wolves, and I was left alone in the night. And I met assassins who ran after me, and I ran, and they followed me, and I ran, and they were still after me, and I ran until they hung me on a branch of the big oak-tree, where the beautiful child with blue hair sent a carriage for me. And the doctors, when they looked at me, said straight away, 'If he isn't dead, it shows that he's alive.' And then I told a lie, and my nose began to grow, so that I couldn't get out of the room. And I went with the fox and the cat for the very purpose of

burying the four gold pieces, for I'd spent one of them at the inn; and the parrot laughed at me, and instead of two thousand gold pieces I didn't find anything; and when the judge heard about it, he put me in jail to please the thieves. And when I left the prison, I saw a bunch of grapes, and I was caught in a trap; and the peasant, who was perfectly right, put a dog collar on me, and made me guard the poultry yard; but he soon found out I was innocent, and sent me away. And the serpent with the smoking tail started to laugh, and broke a blood vessel, and then I came back to the beautiful child's home, but she was dead, and the pigeon saw that I was crying, and said, 'I saw your father making a boat to go after you,' and I said, 'Oh, if only I had wings, too!' and he said, 'Do you want to go to your father?' and I said, '*Do* I? Of course I do! But who will take me?' and he said, 'I will take you,' and I said, 'How?' and he said, 'Get on my back.' And so we flew all night, and when morning came we saw the fishermen looking out over the sea, and they said to me, 'There's a poor man in a tiny boat, who'll soon be drowned.' And I knew you at once, for though you were so far away, my heart told me it was you; and I made signs to you to come back ..."

"I recognized you, too," said Geppetto, "and I would have been glad to come back, but how could I? The waves were so high, and a giant one upset my boat. A horrid shark that was near came towards me as soon as he saw me in the water, and, sticking out his tongue, he swallowed me as if I had been a tart."

"How long have you been shut up in here?" asked Pinocchio.

"It must surely be two years since that day – two years, my Pinocchio, that have seemed like two centuries."

"How have you managed to live here? Where did you find the candle? And the matches to light it? Who gave them to you?"

"If you listen I'll tell you the whole story. In that same storm that overturned my boat, a merchant ship was also sunk. The sailors were all saved, but the ship was lost. The shark had a very good appetite that day, and after he had swallowed me, he swallowed the ship, too."

"What! How did he do it?" asked Pinocchio in amazement.

"All in one mouthful. All that he spat out was the mainmast, because it stuck between his teeth, like a fish bone. Luckily for me, the ship was full of cans of preserved meat, biscuits, bottles of wine, dried grapes, cheese, coffee, sugar, candles, and matches. With all these provisions I have been able to live for two years; but now my supply is exhausted. There is nothing left in the pantry, and the candle you see is the last one."

"And then?"

"And then, my dear, we shall remain in the dark."

"Then, dear daddy," said Pinocchio, "there is no time to lose. We must find a way to escape immediately."

"To escape . . . But how?"

"We might escape through the mouth of the shark, into the sea, and swim away."

"That's all very well, dear Pinocchio, but I can't swim."

"That doesn't matter. I am a good swimmer. You can come on my back, and I'll carry you safely to the shore."

"It's no use, my boy," answered Geppetto, with a sad smile, shaking his head. "A puppet like you, only three feet tall, could not be strong enough to swim if I were on his back."

"Try it, and you'll see!"

Without another word, Pinocchio took the candle, went ahead and showed his father the way, saying to him, "Follow me, and don't be frightened!"

They went like this for some time, through the whole body and the stomach of the shark. When they came to his throat, they stopped to look round, as they wanted to seize the right moment for their flight.

You must know that the shark was very old, and that as he suffered from asthma and palpitation of the heart, he had to sleep with his mouth wide open. So, when Pinocchio reached his throat and looked upwards, he could see a large strip of starry sky, and a big bright moon.

"This is the right moment to escape," he whispered to his father. "The shark is sleeping like a dormouse. The sea is smooth, and it is as bright as day. Come, daddy – come after me, and in a few minutes we shall be free!"

And they did it. They climbed up the shark's throat, and when they were in that huge mouth they passed his tongue on tiptoe. His tongue was as long and wide as a fair-sized garden path. They were just prepared to jump into the sea when the shark sneezed, shaking them so violently that they fell back into his stomach.

Their fall extinguished the candle, and father and son were in the dark.

"Now what shall we do?" said Pinocchio.

"Now, my son, we are lost!"

"Why should we be lost? Give me your hand, daddy, and be careful not to slip."

"Where are we going?"

"We must try again. Come with me, and don't be frightened!"

With these words, Pinocchio took his father's hand, and, all the time walking

133

on tiptoe, again they went up the monster's throat, walked along his tongue, and climbed over the three rows of teeth.

Before jumping into the sea the puppet said to his father, "Now climb on my back, and stick tight. I'll do the rest."

As soon as Geppetto was on his back, Pinocchio jumped into the sea and began to swim. The sea was as smooth as oil, the moon shone brightly and the shark slept so soundly that cannon-fire would not have disturbed him.

CHAPTER 36

At last Pinocchio ceases to be a puppet,
and becomes a real boy

hile Pinocchio was swimming towards the land as quickly as he could, he noticed that his father, sitting on his back with his legs in the water, was trembling violently, as though feverish.

Was he shivering because of cold, or of fright? Who knows? Perhaps a little of both. But Pinocchio thought he was frightened, and he tried to comfort him, "Courage, daddy! In a few minutes, we shall reach land, and be safe."

"But where is this land?" asked the old man, growing more uneasy every moment, and blinking like a sailor threading a needle. "Here I am looking everywhere, and I can't see anything but water and sky."

"But I see land, too," said the puppet. "You know I am like a cat: I see better at night than in the daytime."

Poor Pinocchio pretended to be cheerful, but he was rather discouraged. He grew weaker, and breathed with difficulty; in short he was almost exhausted, and land was still very far away.

He swam until he could breathe no longer: then he turned to his father, and said, "Daddy, help me . . . I am dying!"

Father and son were about to drown together, when a voice, like a badly tuned guitar, said, "Who is dying?"

"I, and my poor father!"

"I recognize your voice! You are Pinocchio!"

"Right. And who are you?"

"I am the tunny fish, your pal in the shark's body."

"How did you escape?"

"I did the same as you, but you showed the way. I followed you, and I, too, escaped."

"Dear tunny, you've come just in time! I beg you, for the love you have for your children, the little tunnies, to help us, or we are lost."

"Of course! With all my heart. Catch my tail, and let me tow you. You will reach land in four minutes."

You can be sure that Geppetto and Pinocchio accepted the invitation at once; but, instead of catching the tunny's tail, they found it better to sit on his back.

"Are we too heavy?" asked Pinocchio.

"Heavy! No, on the contrary, you're light as a feather! It's as if I had two empty seashells on my back," answered the tunny, who was as big and strong as a two-year-old calf.

Reaching land, Pinocchio jumped down first, and then he helped his father. Then he turned to the tunny, and said in a trembling voice, "My dearest friend, you have saved my father's life! I cannot find words to thank you. May I give you a kiss, as a token of my eternal gratitude?"

The tunny put his nose out of the water, and Pinocchio, kneeling on the ground, pressed a loving kiss on its mouth. At this sign of real, unaffected love, the tunny, who was not used to such things, was so moved that, ashamed to be seen crying like a baby, he dived under the water, and disappeared.

Meanwhile, the sun had risen.

Pinocchio gave his arm to Geppetto, who was so weak that he could hardly stand, and said, "Lean on my arm, dear daddy, and let us go. We must walk slowly, like snails; and when we are tired we shall stop and rest."

"And where shall we go?" asked Geppetto.

"We'll try to find a house, or a cabin, where we can ask for a bit of bread, and some straw to make our bed."

They had walked hardly a hundred steps when they noticed by the roadside two ugly faces, waiting to beg of the passers-by.

They were the fox and the cat, but they were so changed that you could hardly have recognized them. The cat had pretended so long to be blind that she really had become blind; the fox had grown old, his fur was entirely moth-eaten on one side, and he had even lost his tail. This had happened because the wretched thief became so poor that one day he had to sell his beautiful tail to a hawker, who wanted it for driving away flies.

"Oh, Pinocchio," sobbed the fox, "give something to two poor invalids."

"Invalids," repeated the cat.

"Good-bye, scoundrels!" answered the puppet. "You cheated me once, but you never will again."

"Believe me, Pinocchio, we are really poor and miserable."

"Poor and miserable!" repeated the cat.

"If you are poor, serve you right. Remember the proverb, 'Easy come, easy go!' Good-bye, scoundrels!"

"Have pity on us!"

"On us!"

"Good-bye, scoundrels! Remember the proverb, 'The devil's flour is all bran'."

"Do not abandon us!"

"Us!" repeated the cat.

"Good-bye, scoundrels! Remember the proverb, 'He who steals his neighbour's cloak, ends his life without a shirt'!"

Speaking thus, Pinocchio and Geppetto went peacefully on their way; but they had hardly gone another hundred steps when they noticed, at the end of a narrow path in a meadow, a charming little cottage made of bricks and tiles, with a roof of straw.

"Someone must live in that cottage," said Pinocchio. "Let us knock on the door."

"Who is it?" said a tiny voice, inside.

"A poor father and his poor son, with no bread, and without a home," answered the puppet.

"Turn the key, and the door will open," said the tiny voice.

Pinocchio turned the key, and the door opened. They went in and looked around, but they saw nobody.

"Where can the house-owner be?" asked Pinocchio in amazement.

"Here I am, up here."

Father and son looked up at the roof, and there on a little crossbeam was the talking cricket.

"Oh, my dear cricket!" said Pinocchio, with a polite bow.

"So I am your 'dear cricket' now, am I? Do you remember when you chased me from your home by throwing a mallet at me?"

"You are right, cricket. Drive me away, too. Throw a mallet at me, too! but for pity's sake don't drive away my poor father."

"I shall have pity on both of you, father and son, but I wanted you to remember the cruel treatment I received. It may teach you that in this world we should treat everyone kindly as far as it is possible, that we ourselves may be treated kindly when we need it."

"You are right, cricket. You are absolutely right, and I'll remember the lesson. But tell me, how did you manage to buy this beautiful cottage?"

"This cottage was given to me yesterday, by a kind goat with beautiful blue hair."

"What has become of the goat?"

"I don't know."

"When will she be back?"

"She will never be back. She left yesterday, very sad, and bleating as if to say, 'Poor Pinocchio, I shall never see him again! The shark must have eaten him by now'!"

"Did she say that? It must have been the fairy – it was surely the fairy – my dear little fairy!" cried Pinocchio, sobbing bitterly, and bursting into floods of tears.

When he had had a good cry, he dried his eyes, and made a good bed of straw for old Geppetto. Then he said to the talking cricket, "Tell me, cricket, where can I get a cup of milk for my poor father?"

"Giangio, the gardener, lives three paddocks away from here. He has some cows. If you go there, you might get some milk."

Pinocchio ran at once to Giangio's house, who asked him, "How much milk do you want?"

"I want a cupful."

"A cup of milk costs a penny. First give me a penny."

"I haven't even a farthing," answered Pinocchio, very sadly.

"That's too bad," answered the gardener. "If you haven't even a farthing, why should I have milk for you?"

"Never mind!" said Pinocchio, and he turned to go away.

"Wait a minute," said Giangio. "Perhaps we can manage it. Will you turn the windlass for me?"

"What is a windlass?"

"It's a machine that carries up water from the well to water the garden."

"I'll try."

"Well, if you will draw a hundred buckets of water, I'll give you a cup of milk."

"I'll do it."

Giangio took the puppet into the garden, and showed him how to turn the windlass. Pinocchio started at once, but before he could draw the hundred buckets of water he was perspiring from head to foot. He had never worked like that before.

"It was my donkey's work until today," said the gardener, "but the poor beast is dying."

"May I go and see him?" asked Pinocchio.

"Certainly."

When Pinocchio came into the stable, he saw a fine donkey on the straw. He was dying of hunger and hard work.

He looked at him, and said to himself, trembling, "I think I know that donkey. His face isn't new to me." And, coming near him he said in ass idiom, "Who are you?"

At this question the dying donkey opened his eyes and answered in the same language, "I . . . am . . . Lamp . . . wick . . ." After which he closed his eyes and died.

"Oh, poor Lampwick!" murmured Pinocchio and, taking some straw, he wiped the tears that were running down his cheek.

"Are you so sorry for this donkey that doesn't cost you anything?" said the gardener. "What shall I do, I who paid for it in hard cash?"

"I'll tell you . . . he was my friend."

"Your friend?"

"Yes, he was a schoolmate of mine."

"What!" shouted Giangio, bursting out laughing. "What! You had an ass for a schoolmate? Fine lessons you must have had in your school!''

The puppet was so shamed by these words that he did not answer, but took his milk and returned to the cottage.

From that day, for over five months, he got up before dawn every morning to turn the windlass, so as to earn the cup of milk for his father. But that was not all; in his spare time, he learned how to weave baskets of reeds. He sold them, and they had enough to pay for all their needs. He also made a fine little cart, in which he took his father for a ride and a breath of fresh air when the weather was fine.

When evening came, he practised reading and writing. For a few pennies he bought a large book in the city, whose index and title page were missing; but it served him very well. He cut a pen out of a small twig and, as he had neither ink nor inkwell, he used a little bottle of cherry and blackberry juice.

Because of his ingenuity and his diligence, his father, whose health was still very bad, could live very comfortably. He even saved two shillings, to buy himself a new suit.

One morning he said to his father, "I'm going to the market today, to buy myself a new jacket, a cap, and a pair of shoes. When I come back," he added, laughing, "I shall be so beautiful that you'll mistake me for a great lord."

He felt very happy and satisfied as he ran along. Suddenly he heard someone speaking to him. He turned and saw a fine snail coming from the hedge.

"Don't you know me?" said the snail.

"Perhaps, but I'm not sure . . ."

"Don't you remember that snail who was the blue-haired fairy's maid? Don't you remember how I came downstairs to let you in, and how I found you with your foot sticking in the door?"

"I remember everything!" cried Pinocchio. "Tell me quickly, dear snail, where did you leave my good fairy? What is she doing? Has she pardoned me? Does she still remember me? Does she love me still? Is she very far from here? Can I go and see her?"

Pinocchio asked all these questions as fast as he could, without once stopping to breathe.

But the snail answered with her usual slowness, "My dear Pinocchio, the poor fairy is sick in a hospital!"

"In a hospital?"

"Unhappily, yes. Harassed by a thousand calamities, she is very, very ill, and she hasn't the money to buy even a tiny piece of bread."

"Is it possible? Oh, how dreadful! Oh, the poor fairy! The poor fairy! If I had a million pounds, I'd give them to her; but I have only two shillings. Take them; I was just going to buy myself a new suit. Take them quickly, snail, to the kind fairy."

"But your new suit?"

"What does a new suit matter? I'd even sell these rags I have on if I could help her. Go, snail, hurry! If you will come back again in two days, I may be able to give you a little more. I've worked until now for my father; from now on, I'll work five hours longer every day, for my kind mother. Good-bye, snail, I'll expect you in two days."

The snail, most surprisingly, began to run like a lizard in summer.

When Pinocchio arrived back, his father asked him, "Where is your new suit?"

"I couldn't find one that fitted me. Never mind! I'll buy it next time."

That evening, instead of working until ten o'clock, Pinocchio worked until midnight; and instead of making eight baskets, he made sixteen.

Then he went to bed, and fell asleep. As he slept, he dreamed he saw the fairy, lovely and smiling, who gave him a kiss, saying, "Brave Pinocchio! In return for your good heart, I forgive you all your past misdeeds. Children who love their parents, and help them when they are sick and poor, are worthy of praise and love, even if they are not models of obedience and good behaviour. Be good in future, and you will be happy."

Then the dream ended, and Pinocchio awoke, full of amazement.

You can imagine how astonished he was when he saw that he was no longer a puppet, but a real boy just like other boys. He looked round; but instead of the straw walls of the cottage, he saw a lovely little room simply though beautifully furnished and papered. He jumped out of bed, and found a pretty new suit, a new cap, and a pair of boots as pretty as a picture.

When he was dressed, he put his hands in his pockets, and found there a little ivory purse on which these words were written: *"The blue-haired fairy returns Pinocchio's two shillings, and thanks him for his good heart."*

He opened the purse, and, instead of two silver shillings, there were twenty gold pieces in it.

Then he went to look in the mirror, but he could not recognize himself. Instead of the usual picture of a wooden puppet, he saw the expressive, intelligent face of a good-looking boy, with brown hair and blue eyes, who looked contented and full of joy.

Amidst all these wonders, Pinocchio no longer knew whether he was awake or asleep with his eyes open.

"And my father, where is he?" he cried, suddenly. He hurried into the next room and there he saw old Geppetto, well, and brisk, and good-natured, as he had been before. He had again taken up his old art of wood-carving, and just then he was planning a beautiful cornice, decorated with leaves and flowers, and animal heads.

"Daddy, tell me, what is the meaning of this sudden change?" asked Pinocchio, hugging and kissing him.

"This sudden change is all due to you," answered Geppetto.

"Why is it due to me?"

"Because when children who were naughty become good, it gives a new smiling appearance to the whole family."

"And the old wooden Pinocchio, where is he?"

"There he is," answered Geppetto, pointing to a large puppet that was leaning against a chair with his head on one side, his arms hanging loosely, and his legs bent and crossed, so that it was a miracle that he could stand there.

Pinocchio turned and looked at him for a moment, and then said to himself, contentedly, "How ridiculous I was when I was a puppet! And how happy I am to have become a real boy!"

THE END

Carlo Collodi was the pen name of Carlo Lorenzini, a famous Italian writer of humble origins who was born in northern Italy in 1826. (He took the name "Collodi" from his mother's birthplace.) He was educated in Florence and although he spent much of his childhood running wild, he trained to become a priest when he left school. After a time he decided he did not have a vocation so he became a journalist, founding his own newspaper and theatrical journal. In 1860 he became a government official with a particular interest in education, and it was at this time he began writing for children. *The Adventures of Pinocchio*, originally written as a serial, appeared in book form in 1883 and quickly sold a million copies in Italy alone. When the book became available in English in 1892, it was greeted with tremendous enthusiasm and has been a great favourite ever since.

67265

Collodi, Carlo

Col

The adventures of
Pinocchio

$19₀₀

4428